Pick Your Poison

Tales of Stella and Jonas
Third Tale in the Series

Pick Your Poison (2018), the third novel by West Virginian Becky Hatcher Crabtree, continues the story of an independent spirit, Stella, and Jonas, her Inupiaq man.

Hungover with Grandma (2016), the second of the series, ranges from West Virginia to Alaska and back with Stella and Jonas's Inupiaq family. **Hungover with Grandma** earned a Forward Indie 2016 Finalist rating for Multicultural Fiction and Feathered Quill 2017 Best Women's Fiction.

Drunk on Peace and Quiet (2015), the first in the series, introduces straight-talking, practical Stella, her troubled brother, Timmy Lee, and the man she loves, Jonas Akpik. **Drunk on Peace and Quiet** was awarded a 2016 Eric Hoffer Honorable Mention for ebook fiction by a small press.

Pick Your Poison finds Stella and Jonas facing the need to fight like never before, to save their land and mountain from greedy and dangerous pipeline destruction. And fight they do. As always, Stella and Jonas have the lingering and real threat on their lives posed by the the truly wicked Timmy Lee. The story weaves two intertwined narratives with courage, humor, adventure, danger — and heart, a West Virginia heart!

—Jay St. Vincent
Associate Professor of English (ret),
Ilisagvik College, Utqiagvik, Alaska

I had a wonderful time inside this story. I believe we have to stand up for what is right and Stella did.

—Anne Phillips
Environmental Activist

Stella's back in fine, feisty form! Crabtree makes good use of her own experience in protesting an encroaching pipeline on her property, intertwining Stella's story with that of her reprehensible brother to wind to a most satisfying conclusion.

—Vicki Lane
Author of the Elizabeth Goodweather
Full Circle Farm Mysteries

An inspiring story about pipeline resistance in Appalachia and one woman's passion for justice. We can all learn from Stella's bold courage as she takes to the trees to defend what she loves. May all those fighting pipelines have her determination and strength!

—Appalachians Against Pipelines

A cleverly written, entertaining and satisfying return to Monroe County and Stella's story. The suspense and excitement along with the strength and love for all Stella holds dear shines through once again!

—Lynda Rogers
Resident, Monroe County, West Virginia

Pick Your Poison

Becky Hatcher Crabtree

Library of Congress Control Number: 2018960582

ISBN 978-1-888215-35-9 (Paperback)

eBook ISBN 978-1-888215-34-2 (e-book)

While the places in this work of fiction may be real or based on real locations, the persons and activities depicted are entirely fictional, are based solely on the author's wild, free-ranging imagination and any resemblance to persons living or dead is purely coincidental. In other words, the author has spun a yarn based on a pack of lies. There's not a word of truth in it.

Fathom Publishing Company
PO Box 200448
Anchorage, AK 99520
https://www.fathompublishing.com
https://www.beckycrabtree.com

Printed in the United States

Dedicated to

the spirit

of strong women

everywhere

who must

make courageous decisions

(picking their poison)

in

difficult situations

Table of Contents

Preface (Nod to Reality)   ix
Acknowledgments   xi
End of Summer   1
Grapes and Retirement   7
Beach Pastor   11
Change   15
Singing on the Pier   17
Lindside Living   21
Beach Life   27
Winter   31
Here Comes the Pipeline   35
Beauty of the Land   39
Back to the Beach – Sea View Nursing Home   43
Follow the Money   47
Pondering the Pipeline   53
Tales of the Pipeline   57
Naomi's Romance   63
Prepping for MTP   67
J. W.   71
Here's the Deal   75
Federal Court   81
Decision from the Judge   85
Springtime in the South   89
Hope of Love   95
Pipeline and Trees   99
Tree-Sitting Eve   103
Tree-sitting   109

First Skirmish   113
Another Day in the Trees   117
And Then There was One   121
Security and Deputies   125
I Never Saw a Moor   131
About Ready to Sing   135
Naomi & Margaret   141
Down Time   145
Sleepover Preparations   149
Vacation Time   153
Ritz Number Five   157
Packing   161
Amazing Atlantic   165
Take Me Home   169
Stella Sees Him   173
Lost and Found   177
Country Roads, Take Me Home   179
Fishing   185
Tractor Lesson   189
After the Boom   193
Identification   195
Epilogue   201
About the Author   203

Preface (Nod to Reality)

This story progressed as our West Virginia property was taken by eminent domain to build a huge natural gas pipeline. Our real-life experiences cast a shadow over my writing as far as court cases and tree-sitting and pipeline construction go.

Another reality was the death of my dog during the writing of this book. Buddy (2007-2018) succumbed on May 17, likely from a heart attack. He was a good dog and his death left a hole in my heart.

The places are all real, South to North from Charleston and Myrtle Beach, South Carolina, to Fancy Gap, Virginia, to Lindside and Pence Springs and Charleston, West Virginia.

All the people depicted and their actions are pure fiction. Any resemblance to persons living or dead is completely coincidental. Frankly, this book is all a big fantasy, happily created in my imagination.

Becky Hatcher Crabtree
September 2018

Acknowledgments

The residents of Monroe County, West Virginia know great stories and I need to thank them all for sharing, especially Betty and John Spangler and their son, Johnny.

Sheldon Brown complained loudly about Timmy Lee being left out in the cold in the last book. His griping got me writing again.

My dear friend, Mr. Harold M. Linkous is a resident at Springfield Center, a nursing home in the mountains of West Virginia. He was kind enough to explain experiences there when I visited.

I am ever indebted to Katie Adkins and Pam Agee Jackson who edited the roughest of manuscripts.

Merri Hess and Jay St. Vincent, as always, encouraged me to keep writing. Merri showed me the sights of downtown Charleston, South Carolina last spring. The unbelievably delicious coconut cake there found its way into the story along with other icons from the area.

Publisher Connie Taylor has worked her magic again. Her patience, knowledge, and experience pull the best from my attempts at writing.

During the past year, we have met some marvelously courageous environmentalists, activists, and journalists around the pipeline. I am very grateful that their paths have crossed mine. Their choices and professionalism have influenced my life more than they will ever know.

Becky Hatcher Crabtree
September 2018

Chapter 1

End of Summer

By September of the next year, Stella barely remembered to lock the door and had quit braking when she saw a flash of movement in the woods lining the back roads. Memories of the horrors Timmy Lee had created came to life less and less often.

Late at night, Stella and Jonas sometimes speculated about Timmy Lee's status.

"Maybe he got hurt when he killed that guy and died ... " Stella often pondered.

"Haven't seen any buzzards circling since he left. If he died, it wasn't around here." Jonas was as practical as his wife.

Stella would almost always follow up by stating, "My brother is too mean to die. He'll live to be a hundred, out there somewhere. He may be done with us. Lordy, I hope so, but he is working his evil somewhere on someone else."

She'd go through the pieces of the puzzle that was Timmy Lee: "The dead man in the barn worked at the Mildred Mitchell-Bateman Hospital where Timmy Lee had been committed. For the life of me, I can't figure out how they were connected, but Lord knows they were." She was usually talking to herself by that point.

Jonas would stir in his almost sleep and throw his strong arm over her, as if he knew she was in a dark place. She would relax and cuddle up to his warm body and feel safe, thanking God that Jonas had come into her life over 30 years ago and had loved her for nearly that long. The worry caused by Timmy Lee was relegated to concrete thinking during waking hours. They slept the deep, hard sleep born of hard work, prayer, and a clear conscience.

Chapter 1

When she awoke, her back pressed against Jonas's chest, Stella whispered her daily prayer, "Thank you for sending Jonas to me. Please keep him safe and help me to do right. Try to help Timmy Lee, Lord, but if you can't, please keep him away from me." Then she would twist herself out of the sheets and get up gradually, sitting on the side of the bed before she ventured down the hall to the bathroom.

The cats and dogs and chickens were waiting to be fed and the sheep and goats needed to be let out of the barn. Coyotes had gotten three lambs in the spring so Stella was vigilant about keeping the sheep locked up at night.

This fall morning, after her morning chores, Stella fixed breakfast for her husband in their spotless farm kitchen, surrounded by sterilized Mason jars sparkling on the counters. Stella was not her usual cheery self. She moped around, going through the motions of an activity that she normally loved, preparing to put up food for winter. Jonas watched from the breakfast table, eating the last crumbs of bacon he'd pressed against the last bite of a biscuit. He sensed that his wife was hurting and that fear might be intruding. Supporting his massive frame on the table as he stood up, he took a step to the sink where she was working. Stella turned to face him and he put his hands on her shoulders. Their eyes met, his dark and unwavering and hers blue and watery, a study in contrasts. "Baby, you gotta let go of Timmy Lee, all the aggravation ... and the fear. He's gone, probably for good." Then he smiled with one corner of his mouth and she glowered, the mood broken.

"What's so funny?"

"Well, seems like you missed two good chances to shoot him, guess now we have to put up with him." Jonas knew the way to reach Stella was to make her mad and then make up. "Maybe you need more target practice with the Pink Lady?"

She pulled free and stamped her foot.

"Oh, you! My gun didn't fire the first time and it was in the church so just as well. I missed the second time because I couldn't see him in the dark. That little red dot didn't help my aim a bit, because I just couldn't see where to put it."

She lowered her head. "But ... as bad as he is, stealing from the church and my friend Anna, and as much trouble as he's caused for me, I'm sorta glad I didn't hit him. Even if he did terrorize me and break into my house. Sometimes I wonder what he would have done to me if I hadn't shot at him."

2

Jonas took her in his arms. "Me, too, Babe, real glad you missed. He'll get his. Living well is the best revenge. And you are nothing if not a survivor." Stella wiped a stray drop of water from her cheek with a dish towel; she'd never admit to a tear.

She looked around the kitchen. "You could come and help me pick grapes. Juice and jelly are the plan for today."

Jonas looked at his watch. "I have to be at work in 45 minutes and it takes 30 to get there."

"So, be late for once in your life." She was thoughtful. "Or better yet, retire. I promise I'll keep you busy around here." She arched an eyebrow and Jonas chuckled.

"I can't retire just yet, but I can be back by mid-afternoon. Wait for me and I'll pick all the grapes for you."

Waving an arm at the empty jars, she spoke, "By the time you get home, these will be full of purple goodness."

"Someday, I'll be able to stay home and help, Baby. Someday."

He tried to get another hug but Stella turned away to grab a basket for the grapes, muttering, "Huh, someday soon would suit me."

"C'mere." Jonas faced off again with his wife. "How about this? I'll get the paperwork from HR and ask about a pension estimate and we can start planning."

Stella hugged him, a full-frontal embrace. "Sounds like a start." She was smiling a lot more on the inside than her face showed when Jonas left for work, the wooden screen door slamming behind him.

The grape arbor, built by Jonas and tended by Stella, was on the other side of the garden. It was hanging full of purple clouds of grapes at the peak of ripeness. They were firm now, deep purple (but not musical) and nearly bursting with juice. Stella had been watching them closely and figured in another day or two they'd start to shrivel. Today was the day to pick.

She gathered her garden shears and basket, ready to work while the grass was still dewy and the morning air felt cool in the shadow of Peters Mountain. A choir of birds watched from the power line, singing their complaints about her intrusion into the arbor. Stella's low spirits flew as she fussed aloud to them, "It's my turn in the grapes, you guys have had them all to yourselves, time to share with me." She hummed with them as she worked, clipping the clusters with her right hand and cradling them gently in her left before placing them carefully in the basket, then she turned to stretch and spoke to the birds

Chapter 1

again, "I won't pick them all, you greedy things, you can have what I leave." She waved her arm at the line of birds and many of them went silent and flew away.

Her elderly dog, Buddy, settled in the grass beside her and, done with the birds, Stella started talking to him. "The vines are mighty full this year, I am pretty impressed." She started trying to remember Biblical references to grapes and explain them to the dog. "Noah grew grapes, must've been one of the first." She picked a few more clusters. "Seems like he was the first one to get drunk off of wine, too, but we don't hear much preaching on that." She chuckled. "In the Bible, grapes are used as symbols of fertility, too, or maybe prosperity." Buddy didn't seem interested, so she hummed some more and snipped dozens more bunches of grapes before she spoke again.

"Old Mrs. McDaniel called them 'the queen of fruit' and showed me how to make grape juice the easy way, and grape jelly, and grape pie. She said grapes cured cancer of the innards and helped keep wrinkles and joint pain away. Buddy, maybe you should have a few, with that arthritis in your hip." She bent over to stroke Buddy's back and he groaned little contented groans. "I never believed any of that stuff, but I sure am glad she taught me how to use the things that grow here. What would I have done without her?"

Stella had run away from her home near Atlanta on the night of her high school graduation, ridden the bus to Bluefield, West Virginia, got a room in a rooming house run by Blanche Boswell, learned accounting at a business college and landed a job in Monroe County. She was to provide live-in care for the ailing, elderly Rachel McDaniel in return for her room and board and the deed to the family farmhouse and twenty acres upon Mrs. McDaniel's death. It was more than a job. Their friendship bloomed and the old lady had taught her some priceless country lore, along with life skills of a different sort – how to live independently. Her son, Ben, was best friends with Jonas Akpik, and he'd sent Jonas up to check on the farmhouse one day. The rest was history. Bumping along, tragic history since Jonas thought he was still married to his teenaged bride. After learning his previous wife had passed away, the romance with Stella had finally evolved happily with their wedding the previous Christmas. Stella felt that she couldn't be any happier, except of course, if Timmy Lee could be corralled and truly out of her life.

Buddy had wandered away and suddenly started yipping and lunging forward and backward at something in the grass. She ambled over and saw his source of annoyance. "Nice one, Bud, biggest black snake I've seen this summer." He backed off, panting, still focused on the snake. There had been a time when Stella would've grabbed it by the tail and cracked it like a whip, but she knew she wasn't as quick as she once was and it was at least seven feet long. She figured she wasn't strong enough to crack it either. "Shouldn't kill something that doesn't need to die, but it does need to relocate."

She found a hoe in a hollow tree near the garden where she kept long-handled tools and led the snake to wind around the business end. She carried it into the ravine nearby to set it free, Buddy supervising. She wiped her face, sweat starting to drip, and replaced the hoe in the old tree.

The sun had risen to nearly overhead and the morning dew had burned off. Stella was feeling her cool skin warming up and getting moist. Her hair was starting to frizz up, little springs of curls were falling out of her ponytail and she knew it was time to quit. Besides, her basket was overflowing, so she tucked away the shears in the hip pocket of her jeans and headed to the back door, a basket on one hip, and an old yellow lab trudging along behind her.

6

Chapter 2

Grapes and Retirement

Some hours later, when Jonas pulled open the back door, he was greeted with the sauna-like sight of a steam-filled, grape-flavored kitchen. The fragrance was so strong that he licked his lips to see if he could taste it. Through the fog, he could see half gallon jars of grape juice lined up near the sink and neat rows of smaller jars on the counter top all full of purple jelly. His eyes drifted around the room and found two lattice top pies on the table, grape pies, he assumed. Stella was struggling with the heavy lid of a pressure cooker, pressure valve still jiggling. He stepped toward her, "Might give that thing a little more

Chapter 2

time, Ma'am, still a lot of pressure build-up." She dropped her arms and wiped her face with a purple-splotched towel.

"You are probably right," she admitted, "but I just have one more load and I was trying to get it all done before you got here."

"Looks like you are on a mission to get scalded. Why don't you let it cool off? We've got all evening."

"Whew, lots of juice and jelly, but no dinner. Gonna be from the freezer tonight, I guess."

"How about a piece of grape pie for an appetizer? Looks like it is calling my name." He reached in the cupboard for two plates. "We have any vanilla ice cream?" He was already at the freezer, looking high and low.

"Look in the door. And grab that box of stir-fry dinner. Might as well get that cooking while the 'appetizer' is served. You've never minded dessert first as I recall."

They retired to the living room to have warm pie and ice cream while dinner cooked. Jonas smacked his lips as he scraped the plate with his fork. "Just right. I like it when the crust is flaky and the filling is still warm."

"A pie connoisseur, are you?"

"Yep." He gathered the plates to return to the kitchen. "Stay put, I have some news."

Stella had pushed the recliner back and had her feet up. "Hit me with your best shot. Night shift? Cutbacks? You've survived it all. What now?"

"Oh, I think you might like this news." Stella pushed the foot of the recliner back in with her heels and sat up.

"What is it?"

"You told me to ask about retirement."

"Yes, I did." Stella spoke slowly and cut her eyes at him as if she wasn't going to believe what he said next.

"Well, I didn't." She fell back in the chair.

"Didn't have to." She sat back up, all ears.

Jonas was clearly relishing the suspense. He took a seat beside her. "Just today, Celanese offered a little retirement buy-out bonus for those who needed a nudge to retire by the end of the year."

Stella felt numb. Could this be the moment she had hoped for? "How much?" She asked the question without feeling in control of her own words or even caring what the answer was.

Jonas slapped his leg. "Enough, Baby, enough."

"When?"

"December 31, if I live. Or, I can retire at the end of September, but my pension will be less. Think I'd like to stay and get loose ends knotted."

She giggled. "Loose ends tied, Jonas, not knotted." Stella rolled her eyes when he confused the phrase as he often did with other sayings, but she soon forgot in the glow of the moment. "Then we could travel or stay up late or ... "

"I had in mind some sleep-ins with my frisky wife, no alarms, and no emergencies at the plant that I have to get up in the night to see about."

"Oh, Jonas, yes, do it, whenever the timing feels right." She fought her way out of the recliner and pulled him by both hands to a hug in the middle of the living room. Then, she started swaying with him and they both drifted into a joint rendition of "I Got You Babe" and a romantic slow dance. For the second time that day, Stella felt like crying.

The absence of a hissing pressure cooker finally got Stella's attention and she broke away to set out the next to last load of jelly and put the last one in the cooker. The frozen stir-fry chicken teriyaki had cooked to perfection even without stirring. As she threw together a meal for them both, she could not keep the grin off her face.

Chapter 3

Beach Pastor

While Stella and Jonas were planning the next big change of their lives together, Timmy Lee, now known as Jonathan Wesley, was starting to strain against the new life he had created in Myrtle Beach, South Carolina. He'd preached all summer and had a small but faithful congregation at the Freedom Chapel, a building that formerly housed "Myrtle's Tees," but it wasn't enough.

Timmy Lee had been a traveling gospel singer all over the southeast for years before moving to Myrtle Beach, the police on his tail. He knew the revival spiel and the words to dozens of gospel songs, so it was an easy transition to sing at a variety of churches and  revivals around the Grand Strand. An evangelist named Patsy Perkins had heard him sing, reached out to him and set him up in what had been a t-shirt store near the beach. He lived in a small room in the back and had worked hard to convert the storefront to a chapel, even building a steeple from thrown-away pallets.

Chapter 3

Most of his furnishings were curbside bargains. From the refrigerator and microwave in his living quarters to the benches in the tiny sanctuary, he was equipped with the castoffs of others. Tourists and college kids threw out a lot of valuable stuff. He'd even sold some of it to make money to buy food and a better wardrobe. At first, he was satisfied. It was a good feeling to forage, make something out of nothing, and come out ahead.

* * * * *

Sitting on the beach early this Sunday morning, his eyes shaded from the rising sun with his hand, he watched the angry Atlantic waves curl up and fall over, crash, and spread out in a soft fan of water. *Just like my life,* he thought. He never tired of watching the waves. *Anger, fight, and get over it. Anger, fight, and get over it.* In real life, the cycle never varied either and as he aged, he was starting to get exhausted with it.

His life was currently in the "get-over-it" stage after a particularly nasty family event. A murder, in fact. His sister's friend, Anna, had been found dead and he had been charged with her murder. A faked nervous breakdown led to his commitment to a mental hospital, Mildred Mitchell-Bateman Hospital. He had escaped and gone looking for revenge on his sister, Stella, her husband, Jonas. Jonas's mother and aunt from Alaska were visiting and even though he'd never met them, he had added them to his list of targets. The escape had been made possible with the help of a nursing assistant in the hospital. An unfortunate meeting between the two several weeks later had resulted in the man's stabbing death at Timmy Lee's hand when he lost control. That was the anger phase, the rising wave and subsequent crash. Now, he was being sought as a suspect in that killing. He was guilty; he accepted that fact within himself but had no intention to admit it to others or serve time because of it. The anger that was starting to rise fed off of his feeling that there were others who were also guilty but had gotten off scot-free. He felt his sister, Stella, was one. Lately, she had been in the middle of everything that had gone wrong for him.

He had escaped in the dead man's car, started singing gospel music again and preaching; building a new life complete with a new name, Jonathan Wesley. *Couldn't beat Wesley for a Methodist name*, he'd thought. People began to come to his chapel. The members of the little congregation were downtrodden, most had hit bottom, but they always responded to his plea to "give

12

so others can hear the glory of God's promises." The offering plate was never empty.

He rose and dusted off the seat of his beige linen slacks. He figured God's promises looked more real if the preacher was well dressed. He'd searched the second-hand stores for brand name men's fashions.

His feelings of contentment had been wavering. He could feel little jolts of jealousy and anger tweaking his thoughts. Now, when it was time to get to his church to preach, he would rather stay at the beach a few more hours, but he had a schedule. One hour a week he had a regular performance. His sister didn't have to report anywhere, why should he?

"Pastor" Wesley strolled back to the little chapel along warm sidewalks lined with flowering shrubs and palm trees. Fitness nuts were already running and dog nuts were walking their animals. He nodded to each person he met, putting on the happy face of a deeply religious man. At least, what he thought a deeply religious man should look like. One of the few people he didn't lie to was himself and he knew he was again using God to make money. Before the service, he wiped the grit of sand from the folding chairs in the tiny sanctuary, shined the podium and straightened the paintings of Christ that he'd gotten at a Goodwill. All part of the Jesus show.

The congregation started to arrive about 9:30 for the 10:00 service. He visited with three young women wearing a lot of makeup, bling, and tight clothing. *Had they even changed from their Saturday night working attire?* The three working girls lived together in a converted garage. He knew this from following them home one Sunday and he'd later seen them working the corner of Ocean Boulevard near the hotels. He felt superior to them, but catered to them because he knew he might need them sometime in some unknown capacity. There was also a teenage runaway with her baby. He didn't know her story, except that home was in Pennsylvania. A Mexican family with four children filled the back row of chairs. The children were the best English speakers in the family and the oldest, a ten-year-old girl, translated for her parents.

Finally, just before ten o'clock, a family of tourists came through the door. That was his bread and butter, tourists exploring a new church to take a bulletin from a beach church back home and maybe putting some cash in the offering plate for whatever reason: guilt from beach pursuits of tanned bodies or booze, pity at the rundown status of the chapel, or maybe a glimpse of redemption through his words. There were a few present most Sundays and they were generous when the offering plate was passed.

Myrtle Beach had certainly opened doors; the rotating tourist congregation had financed some of Timmy Lee's growing needs. He longed for the cash that would provide him with a car, which would in turn elevate his lifestyle and his morale. He'd picked up a gig at the Sea View Nursing Home singing once a week. He hoped that would bring in enough money until he hit the yet unknown jackpot.

Chapter 4

Change

Both Stella and Jonas thought often about his upcoming retirement. It was their new topic of pillow talk, late at night and early in the mornings. It was freeing for Stella to voice her joy as well as her concerns aloud.

"It feels so good to be able to talk about you retiring," she shared as her head lay against his shoulder one morning. "I was kinda afraid to bring it up before. Didn't want to be pushy."

"Shoot, Stella, when were you ever worried about being pushy? You can push with the best of them, sometimes so slick that nobody knows you're pushing."

She turned and smoothed the hair standing up from a cowlick at the crown of his head, then snuggled against him. "Some folks say change is hard, Jonas. How hard is this going to be?"

"As easy or as hard as we want it to be, I reckon. Might be exciting." He tightened his arm around her. "Ben told me a story about his great uncles one time. They lived up here on Peters Mountain and they wanted to see the first car in Lindside. They heard it was coming through one morning on Route 219, but their daddy wouldn't let them take the horses to go down to the main road because he was plowing. He let them go, but they would have had to walk. Then, he explained that they were not going to make it in time to see the car. One of the teenagers turned to the other and said, 'Waal, we can at least see the tracks in the road where that car has been.' The boys took off and spent a half a day to see those tire tracks in the dirt. So, don't tell me change is not exciting!"

Stella had her own story to add. "I hadn't been here long when the first two-part house got moved into Lindside. People lined up to watch it get set up like it was the Fourth of July parade. None of us had ever seen a modular house before. The Poteets, I think it was, had bought the two-part house and Mrs. Poteet told the crowd that if the marriage didn't last, it would be really convenient: she could take her half and he could take his, already separated out. People laughed really hard at that. That house is still there in Lindside, too. People do enjoy a change, sometimes, don't they?"

"Yes Ma'am, I think we'll get used to it. Probably be things come along that we don't expect, good and bad, but we'll figure them all out as we come to it." He paused then looked at the alarm clock. "Good Lord, Stella, I gotta scoot or I won't have a job to retire from." He threw back the covers and gently slapped her thigh as he freed himself from the entanglement of her arms and legs.

Stella moved slowly to get herself up and downstairs to fix a quick breakfast for Jonas. She hadn't even changed out of her nightgown. There was something cozy lazy about being up and doing still in a nightgown. She put coffee on and poured a little glass of juice in one of Mrs. McDaniel's Fostoria tumblers and started heating the griddle for pancakes.

Chapter 5

Singing on the Pier

After church that day, Pastor Wesley returned to the beach, now full of Labor Day visitors. Summer was ending and he knew that the fall would bring a dwindling population: some sport fishermen maybe, and retirees enjoying the mild weather. The families that saved all year for a week of spending money on expensive restaurants and amusement parks wouldn't be back until next summer. He'd miss those tourists. Even though he knew the beach cycle of people, the expected income reduction still sparked angry thoughts.

He decided to walk the beach to clear the darkness in his head. He nodded and greeted everyone he met, knowing that he could sometimes beat back depression by seeming happy.

Chapter 5

"Hello, beautiful day, isn't it?" "Good Morning." "Have a blessed day." When he reached an empty stretch of beach, he sat on the dunes and chewed on a grass stem. Maybe he should go farther south where the season was longer; Florida, maybe. Or even Central America. He'd heard Costa Rica had beautiful white beaches. *I can never get a passport,* he realized, and then refused to give up. *Or maybe I can.* He vowed to himself to explore the options of fake paperwork. There should be some "artist" in Myrtle Beach that could create a social security card and a birth certificate so he could get a driver's license and a passport. He had no documents to confirm his new name but he also possessed nothing to confirm his old name. Even though his fingerprints were probably on file in the podunk Monroe County, West Virginia. If he could get papers in his new name, it would take a while for him to be suspected and even longer to match his fingerprints. Maybe the working girls would know somebody. He would just have to be careful.

The new plan cheered him. He got up and began walking with a new strength in his stride. The pier at Garden City was still several miles away, but he could make it before dark and maybe get a ride home later.

* * * * *

Sitting on the sandy pier stairs a few hours later, Timmy Lee was feeling his age in achy feet and screaming calf muscles. Getting old made him angry, too, didn't seem fair for him to age. The karaoke music from the pier soon caught his attention and distracted him from the latest complaint and, after he sat a while, he trudged up to the outdoor bar to listen where he could see the singers.

As he listened to the tourists taking turns at the mike, he became eager to sing himself. When singers went off key or missed an ending note, he cringed and assured himself that he was so much better than anyone else there. He longed to take the microphone and go into entertainment mode. But he held back. What if someone knew that he was a preacher? Would it be appropriate for a preacher to sing karaoke? What could he sing? Some upbeat CCR or Rolling Stones? He could almost feel the warmth of the metal microphone in his hand, and when he closed his eyes he could hear the applause and the crowd shouting for more. All for him.

"Sir, Sir, are you okay?" He opened his eyes to a tanned teenage waitress with a tray of empty glasses and bottles. She looked relieved, but quickly covered her concern, "Can I get you a drink?"

"Sure, Honey, bring me a Miller Light." Probably be okay for a Myrtle Beach preacher to have a beer, he rationalized. He had no intention of paying for it, but had no plan at the moment as to how to stiff the girl. She was a bleeding heart, an easy target. He figured she needed a lesson on trusting the public. "Start me a tab?"

"Sure, Mister." She made her way through the wooden tables and people to the bar, the hip pockets on her cutoff jeans twisting as she moved. Timmy Lee watched and liked what he saw.

* * * * *

Several beers later, Timmy Lee had decided that Jesus would approve of him singing karaoke as long as it was gospel songs, and he further rationalized that Jesus drank wine so he wouldn't mind a couple of beers for the gospel singer to loosen up. He sang a rousing version of "Do, Lord" amidst foot tapping and hollered "Amens" from the crowd. Their applause strengthened his resolve to sing and he belted out a heart-rending version of "The Old Rugged Cross." He fell right back into his well- worn traveling gospel singing routine, alternating upbeat contemporary tunes with older slow, sweet songs. Even the words of spiritual encouragement came back to him, and as the songs loaded on the karaoke machine, he spoke to the growing crowd. After an entire set of eight songs, he handed the microphone back, wiped the sweat from his forehead and took a cold beer that was offered him. As he returned to his seat, people shook his hand and slapped him on the shoulder.

The young waitress leaned over and whispered, "Tab is paid, Honey. You wowed them." Timmy Lee grinned and sipped his drink and watched the next singers perform. The crowd started to thin as ten o'clock approached, and the emcee, starting to get desperate for a singer, offered Timmy Lee the mike. He waved it off, "Thank you, man, but I need to look for a ride and get on home."

"Come on back next Sunday night, Mister, enjoyed your voice. Where you heading?"

"Up to Myrtle, my ride left me," Timmy Lee lied, knowing that would cause less suspicion than the truth, that he did not have a car.

Chapter 5

After talking to someone behind the bar, the emcee motioned Timmy Lee over and introduced him to an employee who was heading up to Myrtle Beach to pick up his girlfriend after work. The young man was willing to give him a ride. As they talked, he watched his waitress in the background, wiping the bar and smiling at him. *Old enough to be her grandpa,* he thought to himself, and resisted the urge to wink at her. He couldn't stop from giving her his best grin, though, and playfully shooting at her with his finger before he turned to follow the guy to the parking lot.

Stretched out safely in his own cot back at the chapel, he relived the happy moments of glory while he sang: the applause and whooping and praise. *That is when I should've given credit to God,* he thought. *But it wasn't God, it was all me.* He felt dissatisfaction and anger rising, the need to do more and get more: more recognition, more money, more adulation. It took hours of tossing and turning before he finally slept.

Chapter 6

Lindside Living

As Timmy Lee, now Jonathan Wesley, slept two blocks from the Atlantic Ocean, Stella and Jonas were nearly five hundred miles away in the mountains of West Virginia, rising early to get ready for the workweek. "The weather is turning cooler," Stella yawned as she pulled on a sock. "But wasn't this weekend beautiful?"

Jonas rolled over in the bed and rubbed his fingers up and down Stella's back. "Yep, hoping it's the beginning of Indian summer. I could use a few more evenings to cut wood."

"That reminds me, Brooke and Charlene said they were needing a load of firewood. If we have enough, can we take them a load? I can throw it in the pick-up if you'll back it down by the woodpile."

"We have plenty. You checked on them lately? Seems like they are doing okay on their own without their mom. Their mama would be proud of them, getting ready for winter in advance. Always glad to haul to them, what do they call it, bro pono firewood?

21

Probably ought to check their flue and chimney, too. Anna's little house would sure burn fast if there was a chimney fire."

Stella turned and hugged him before crawling back into bed to snuggle. "I love you, even your whacky word flips." She kissed him on both cheeks. "And I love living here in Lindside. People really do care about each other."

Jonas scooted up to a sitting position in the bed and smoothed her flyaway hair back from her face with both hands and held her. After a few seconds, he asked, "Did you hear about the postmistress calling all around to find old Mr. Martin?"

"How come?" Stella raised her head from his chest and sat up. "Is he okay?"

Jonas laughed. "Oh, he's fine, but half the county was looking for him for about an hour. He always picks up his mail every morning at ten o'clock, right after they finish putting it in the post office boxes. Then, he visits with folks in the lobby and in the parking lot. But on Monday he didn't come. The girls kept an eye on his mailbox until eleven o'clock and the mail didn't move. Sometimes he sends a grandkid in to get it, but his mail stayed put. Joyce got a bad feeling and called him. No answer. Then, she called his daughter, no answer. Then, she called 911." He started to laugh again.

"Well, what happened? Tell me." She slapped his chest lightly.

"Okay, okay. He had a doctor appointment in Princeton and his daughter took him up there. Whoever was on the switchboard at 911 knew the number of the mother of the boy who was dating Mr. Martin's granddaughter. The boy's mother had the girl's mother's (Mr. Martin's daughter's) cell number, so they finally reached her in the waiting room of the doctor."

"Oh, mercy! What did she say? What did dear old Mr. Martin say?"

"Word is that it was his best argument for not going into assisted living." Jonas chuckled. "The purpose of the trip was for the daughter to get the doctor to help convince him to live with her or get a room at Country Living or the Springfield Center."

"And is he?"

"Shoot, no. He went up to the Post Office to thank Joyce and promised to call when he wasn't going to be there on time so she wouldn't worry."

"I love it. Living on your own terms is just easier when other people care. I hope we can always do that, too."

She righted herself and pushed out of bed, "How about pancakes for breakfast?" Without waiting for the answer she knew was coming, she added, "I'll start the sausage then go on out and feed the dogs."

She pulled a sweatshirt on over her t-shirt and Jonas spoke, "Pancakes sound good. Hey, c'mere for a minute and look at this thing on my neck. Is it too late for ticks? Feels like a tick." He rubbed his neck. Stella walked around the end of the bed and was gently feeling his neck with both hands when he grabbed her up. She shrieked as he swept her to the side, held her in his arms and buried his face in her neck, kissing it over and over.

"Oh, you! Aren't you tricky today?" She rearranged her hair that had pulled loose from the ponytail and shook her finger at him, where he lay on the bed laughing.

"Jonas Akpik, you behave yourself," then she hurried downstairs.

In a few minutes the smell of sausage persuaded Jonas to start to get up and face the aches and pains he was feeling more often. *Dang knee is bothering me worse as the weather gets cooler and now this shoulder is acting up.* Jonas rubbed it as he sat up on the side of the bed. *Doc said I shouldn't use it for lifting. Guess it got tweaked lifting Stella just now.* He stood, testing the bad knee. *I gotta remember to check today on how much pension I'd lose if I retire now instead of waiting until the end of the year. Sometimes, money isn't worth the cost. Sure would like to finish a project or two at the plant before I leave. Those new guys have never worked anywhere but bossing. Gotta make them understand what our guys are working on and how to keep them safe. Those big shots talk about safety but they don't understand the practical ways to make it happen.* He limped to the bathroom.

Buddy came running when Stella opened the back door. She rubbed his head and fed him dry food in the back yard. She patted the cat and shook out a little can of Fancy Feline moist food for her. Tannie had been throwing up her dry food lately, which made Stella wonder if cats had stomach bugs that left quickly or if she would need a trip to the vet. She put the dish of food on the woodhouse floor so the big fluffy cat could eat undisturbed. Tannie was so desperate to be petted that she arched her back and rubbed against Stella's leg rather than eating. Jonas had cut a small, square hole in the

Chapter 6

woodhouse door as a cat entrance because the dogs enjoyed cat food even more than the cat. *Every creature should be able to eat in peace*, Stella thought as she stroked the cat's fur. Then she remembered the sausage, still on the stove, and hurried back inside.

Jonas was at the stove. "It's okay, Hon, I like them crispy." He was moving the patties onto a paper towel to absorb the extra grease.

Stella washed her hands and readied the milk and flour to make gravy. "The time just got away from me outside." She added flour to the skillet. "It's hard to hurry when your pets want a little attention."

"Oh, that's a good line for getting to work late, too. How should I tell the boss?" His voice became apologetic, "It's hard to hurry when your wife wants a little attention." He turned to look at her, eyebrows arched as if to question if she wanted his attention.

"Jonas, you are so bad. Stand aside so I can make gravy or you might really be late." He took a position behind her and nuzzled her neck as she worked until she gave up and opened her arms for a big smooch. His lips met hers so softly that she felt dizzy and, as always, she was lost in his kiss for a few seconds. She came back to reality when the gravy bubbled and spattered on her arm. "Jonas, the gravy!" She grabbed a potholder and moved the cast iron skillet off the eye. They fixed their plates and ate in silence, both hoping his retirement came sooner rather than later.

Stella spent the day at her desktop computer, updating accounts from six businesses, her clients for over twenty years. Her home bookkeeping service had kept food on the table and paid the power bill after Mrs. McDaniel passed away. She paused a moment from her work to miss her and to offer up her gratitude for the farming lessons and the life lessons. Stella had loved the old woman dearly.

It had been a fairy tale ending, if delayed, to her troubled previous life. Stella had grown up near Atlanta on a dairy farm. Her father had been killed in the barn in a loader accident, and her older brother, Timmy Lee, had bullied and tormented her and their mother until she saw no way out except to run. She believed that God had a hand in the path her life took, because it had all turned out better than she could have planned.

Timmy Lee was her only worry, but he was a big worry. Two years ago, he reappeared and worked as a fundraiser for her church, tried to steal Anna, her best friend's, house and was charged with Anna's murder. He pretended to be insane and was committed to a mental hospital, but escaped and killed a nurse who had helped him get out. Stella was fairly sure that he had killed their mother, too, and had certainly misidentified a drowning victim, telling officials that the body was hers so that no one ever looked for her.

She wondered, for the millionth time, *where is he at this moment: hospital, jail, morgue?* It gave her a chill and she rubbed both arms as she stared at the monitor screen. The thought that always followed ran through her mind again, *what would I do if we meet again?* She had shot at him twice, as Jonas reminded her from time to time, and she alternately felt glad and sad that she had missed. So, she played the "What if" game with herself. *What if he knocked on the back door this minute? Would I let him in or shoot at him through the door? Or call the sheriff? Or what?* She leaned back and tried to be logical. *Buddy would remember Timmy Lee and bark and carry on so that the cowardly man would never even get to the door. Good,* she thought, reassured, and sat up straight to finish entering numbers.

Chapter 7

Beach Life

Jonathan made a couple more trips to the Garden City Pier, sang some, and let folks buy him beers. He developed at least a nodding relationship with the young waitress, who backed off when she saw that he was more a bum than the wealthy older man he pretended to be. Even though he kept up the front, he felt her rejection behind his smiling appearance, and quit going. It was a long walk, too, reminding him how much he needed money to buy a car.

The offering plate at his church was bringing in less money as temperatures dropped and tourists quit coming to the beach. With them gone, other businesses suffered and his congregation of working girls and construction workers also thinned out.

Motivated by his need for money, Preacher Jonathan's sermons at the chapel were beginning to include some fiery warnings about giving.

"God expects a tenth of your income every week!" He slapped his open hand on the podium hard enough to startle a sleeping baby and cause a woman on the back row to pause her jaw momentarily as she noisily chewed her gum. "Look at all the beauty around us. God provides it all – the skies, the oceans, the miracle of life." He moved to the center aisle, his outstretched arm moving to include the congregation and seemingly all outdoors through the tiny windows. "He gives us much." Jonathan turned to walk back to the front, then quickly turned, finger pointing at the people, roaring, "But what he gives, he can take away!" He paused, fire in his eyes. The baby started crying. "Don't displease him through your mortal greed." His last words were soft and he looked at the offering plate and at the picture of Jesus above it. "Amen," he shouted to a silent room.

Sweat trickled down the valley of his spine as he passed the offering plate to the few listeners. As he watched, the back door clicked and he looked up. The woman in the back had slipped out. A Mexican man took the plate and shrugged at his wife before passing it on. Their children each quietly added a quarter to the offering. The preacher led the Doxology, staring at the meager offering centered on the rickety table that served as an altar.

The next Sunday morning, no one came to hear him speak. He was enraged. He ripped the picture of Jesus off the wall and raved and ranted, blaming God, Jesus, and every disciple he could remember for the empty chairs. The pressure and anger grew in his mind. As he tossed and turned that night, he could feel the immediate need to do something. He got up in the night and walked the beach, imagining breaking into one of the few businesses still open in the off season or mugging one of the other people out in the middle of the night.

No, he disciplined himself. *That would be a quick payoff, but maybe not enough money for the risk.* He fought off his urges, commanding himself to *wait for big bucks at the nursing home.* Resolved to have patience and perfect some scam with the elderly, he decided to devote several hours a day to volunteering at the nursing home. *Something has to break for me soon.*

* * * * *

He was eager to get up each day and go to the Sea View Nursing Home. It was all volunteer work, of course, but he was excited by the potential. He hated the smell of the place and refused to interact much with those less fortunate people sitting in their wheelchairs in the hallway, heads lolling about, muttering to themselves or staring at something no one else could see. Still, he was so happy to be there that he nodded a greeting to each of them.

He learned that there were a lot of coherent elderly people with one foot in the grave. They were key to the plan he was developing. First, he memorized the nameplates on the doors and tried to match the names with patients. He noted the ones that never seemed to have visitors, observed them carefully and was helpful to them.

Several days into his plan, an overworked nurse's aide, Paula, stopped him in the hallway with a mailbag of envelopes. "Hey, Reverend Jonathan, I am swamped today. Could you deliver mail to the rooms?"

The preacher turned on the charm. He liked that Paula treated him with respect. He didn't correct the Reverend title. "Of course, I'd be happy to help." *Jackpot of information,* he thought. *Names and return addresses will show somebody with money, someone without close relatives.* He began delivering mail several times a week. Paula was pleased to have more time for other more pressing duties and Preacher Jonathan was closer to his goal. First, he compiled a list of those who never got mail, thinking they would be prime targets. Then he realized that they probably had a next-of-kin taking care of their business, so he changed tactics. He wanted someone who still controlled his or her own bank accounts.

He quickly scanned every envelope he delivered for those from a bank or those that looked like checks, especially stock dividend checks. He looked for oversized plain envelopes for credit cards. *How easy it would be to slip one in my pocket, but no,* he cautioned himself against rushing the plan. *The bigger, better way is for them to give me the money. Patience, man, patience.*

This routine continued for several weeks. Every weekday morning found him at Sea View. He resented and felt betrayed by his absent chapel "flock" but still showed up on Sundays just in case the sponsor showed up. *Who needs 'em anyway? Someone at the nursing home is pure gold and I'm getting closer,* he thought.

In the staff room over coffee, Paula chatted with him while she worked on whatever assignment she had. Today was filling in the calendar of events. Chewing on her pen as she scheduled the events on a clipboard chart, Paula looked up and asked, "How about if we add your singing to the daily schedule this week? Man, you can sing; the residents sure enjoy it. And so do I."

"Glad to hear it, just another service from your local clergy." He wondered if Paula might be a better mark, but decided she was too young and worked too hard to have big bucks.

She met his eyes and it rattled Jonathan a little bit. He wasn't used to sincerity and real praise. After an awkward, too-long pause, he spoke, "I'd be glad to sing, maybe turn it into a sing-a-long. The old folks seem to enjoy the old traditional hymns." She nodded and added the sing-a-long to the afternoon. He practiced a few vintage favorites that night, simple tunes like "Do Lord" and "Rock of Ages" and "Amazing Grace." He had thirty minutes a day, enough time to sing ten hymns at most.

And so, "Music with Jonathan" was born and lived at three o'clock every weekday and Sunday evenings at five o'clock.

After each session, he shook hands and helped nurses wheel patients back to their rooms or to the sunroom. Soon, he became the darling of the breakfast room, where the piano was located. Women old enough to be his mother flirted with him, smiling and looking at him coyly, their rouge and lipstick big and bright. *Like old apple doll clowns,* he thought. His mind raced until he deliberately focused on his mantra: *Find the perfect mark, a lonely old coot that wants to donate money to my church.* He watched the participants closely and showered attention and kindness on all of them. *You just never know,* he thought.

In late November, the patience paid off; he hit a double jackpot. One of the lady residents who arrived with her friends every afternoon to sing got two bank account statements. Not just any bank, but the First National Bank of Peterstown. His hand froze when he saw the familiar blue and red diamond logo in the return address. His sister lived near there, up in West Virginia, and Peterstown was only a dozen miles from Lindside where he'd killed a man over a year ago.

"Are you all right, John?" Paula touched his arm. "Do you need to sit down?"

He barely heard her voice through the roar in his head. "Just a little light-headed." He regained his composure quickly and looked upward while he raised one hand over his eyes and dropped the envelopes to his side with the other hand, covering the return address with his fingers. "Must be these bright lights. I'll be fine." He leaned against the wall and took a deep breath. "Didn't eat breakfast," he lied. "I guess I need something in my stomach."

She led him to the staff room and opened an orange juice. "This'll help. Take a break for a few minutes and let the sugar hit you before you get back to work – hey, let me deliver the mail today."

She reached for the stack, but he smiled and held them out of her reach. "Feeling better already. Thanks, anyway."

"No problem. Take care of yourself, will ya? Good help is hard to find. Especially when it's free." She left him then to continue on her never-ending rounds of caring for the elderly patients.

Jonathan searched through the stack to find the long letters he'd slid into a hiding place between the square ones containing cards. Today's find was golden. He knew the recipient; no one ever visited her. Jonathan Wesley sang inside his head, *Naomi Waterman, Naomi Waterman, Naomi Waterman,* as he placed both letters inside his shirt.

Chapter 8

Winter

October had come and gone, the leaves fell and the warm mountain forest colors became the dreary black and grey of winter to come. The days were cool enough that woodstoves were fired up nearly every day. Jonas had used the few warm evenings they were granted to cut wood for Anna's daughters and grandchildren.

Stella tended Anna and Mrs. McDaniel's graves in the Bradley cemetery one crisp evening during November. It was an awkward time for flowers, not time for the shiny greens and red of Christmas holly yet, but fall was pretty much over. She'd found some dark orange and brown chrysanthemums at the Dollar Store and replaced the faded summer bouquets.

She spoke aloud to her friend as she arranged the plastic flowers in the vases on the headstone, "Anna, your girls are okay. Jonas and I stacked two pick-up loads of wood for them last week." She rose up and stretched, put her gloves back on, and spoke again, "Sugar Bowl better keep his grimy paws off these flowers." She laughed, then half sat on the gravestone and looked down over the valley. Little streams of wood smoke from chimneys wiggled upward with the wind and combined high in the sky. "I wonder how you are doing, Anna." Stella turned and knelt on one leg, grimacing with the effort. "I know you still exist, somehow I am sure of that. You know I hear you laugh sometimes or hear an old saying that you said a lot. Or is heaven different? Do all our spirits combine like the smoke in the valley?" She closed her eyes a moment, then rose and sighed and brushed off Anna's name on the headstone, then that of her husband. "Hey, Charles, hope you are doing okay, too."

Chapter 8

Stella went on to tend old Mrs. McDaniel's grave a few rows over, noting that her son, Ben, good-hearted and well intentioned that he was, had not visited her grave lately. Dead weeds were poking up around the marker. Stella pulled them all up out of the cold mud and threw them over the hill. She kissed her own palm and touched it to the McDaniel name etched into the stone, then blew a kiss toward Anna's grave and hiked back to the road to her waiting Subaru.

She turned the car radio off and drove home in sad silence. Seemed fitting for her mood. As she topped the next hill heading home, the sunset glowed red in front of her. Stella brightened, "Ah, Anna, thanks." By the time she parked her car and petted the dogs, her mood had improved.

"About time you got back, thought I might have to call the fire department and report you lost." Jonas had the oven door open and was pulling out drawers searching for a pot holder to retrieve something from the rack. "Where do you keep the hot pot holders? Need one. Quick."

Stella found one instantly and put it in his hand. "The cornbread is perfect, gotta get it out," Jonas told her.

Stella laughed. "Perfect, huh? How'd you do that?"

"New plan. I used a mix. 'Spiffy' or something like that."

"What? You used a mix for cornbread? Why, there's nothing to it, meal, flour, sugar and baking powder, well, and salt and milk." She was standing with hands on her hips surveying the mess on the counter when it hit her. "What's wrong with my cornbread? Since when do you want it done a new way? Dang it, Jonas, all you had to do was tell me." She watched him grab the hot skillet handle and carefully set it on top of the stove.

"Ben told me about this Spiffy thing at work and I decided to try it out. Looks good, doesn't it?" He turned to his wife, and pointed to the golden-brown top.

"Jonas, you've never cooked anything you didn't have to, ever, in the whole time we've known each other. Why now? Is my cornbread so bad it drove you to cooking?" She pulled out a kitchen chair and flopped down, arms crossed stiffly.

Tossing the pot holder to the top of the stove, Jonas reached for her but she moved just out of reach. He sat down beside her, and pulled her close. "Baby, Baby, there is nothing wrong with your cornbread." He was close to laughing but held back.

"Then why?" Stella re-crossed her arms and faced him eye to eye.

"Well," his words were slow in coming as his mind raced to find the right words to make her understand. "You know I am thinking about retiring. And I am a little scared. Scared to death that I might not know what else to do, that I will be a pain to you here." Stella's eyebrows knitted in bewilderment and her arms fell to her lap. "So, so I thought that I needed to be able to do things around here to help and Ben told me this was an easy way to make cornbread. You like cornbread, right?" Stella nodded, still looking at him, waiting for more explanation. He gave her a quick squeeze then jumped up. "Let's butter it and see what it tastes like."

Stella sat motionless until he sat down with two steaming wedges of cornbread on paper towels, butter dripping from the edges. She took it and watched as he sat back down beside her, blowing on the cornbread to cool it enough to take a bite.

"Jonas, do you mean to tell me that of all the things that need to be done on this farm that you know perfectly well how to do, you have decided to learn how to cook?" Her shoulders started to shake with laughter before the cackles were heard aloud.

He watched for a few seconds, and then joined in. They laughed together until they could speak again. "It felt right at the time, Stella. I swear it did." He noticed a laughter tear on her cheek which she rubbed off against his flannel covered shoulder. Then they sat on the couch silently, shoulders pressed together.

"You okay?" Stella turned his face to her with a hand.

He spoke seriously, "I am getting old, Stella. I'm leaving the best paying job I've ever had and it worries me. It's scary." He studied her face.

Stella was sober when she spoke. "I lived on just my bookkeeping money for years. With that plus your pension, we should be fine." Jonas hung his head. "Better than fine, Jonas."

"Having second thoughts, Stella. I think we ought to upgrade our vehicles while I am still working, we won't have good credit without my job. And, aww, Stella, I wanted to travel, show you the world and go to flea markets and concerts and plant some trees here on the place, maybe an orchard with cherries and apples." He held his head in his hands.

"I never needed a credit check to buy my Subaru from that guy in Rich Creek." She thought a second. "What else? All we need to travel is gasoline. And you can have an orchard for a couple hundred dollars." He ventured a glance at her, met her cold stare, and braced for what was to come. "Humph, sounds to me like you are getting greedy." She surrounded one of his hands with hers. "Me, too. I want more and more of your time."

He moaned and kissed her and sighed, his face still against her. "You are a hard woman, Stella Akpik, but you are right. I'll get over my cold feet soon." He pushed himself upright and grabbed his jacket as he left through the back door.

Stella smiled in spite of herself. She had known that retirement wasn't in his nature and that he would need to be busy when he stopped working, but travel, concerts, and an orchard? *Really? Who could figure out the minds of men?* She went to fix plates of beans and cornbread for them both. She figured he'd be back from his walk before she was finished. She was right; he came inside along with a blast of cold air and a halting apology, restored and ready to proceed with retirement plans.

Chapter 9

Here Comes the Pipeline

One chilly morning in early December, Buddy was barking and carrying on enough to cause Stella to get up from the recliner and look out the window. There was a sparkling white F-350 Ford pickup truck in the yard with a roly-poly man crawling down from the driver's seat, a folder of papers in hand. She watched him edge past the barking dog to the back door. He knocked and knocked while Stella brushed crumbs off the tablecloth and put away some dishes out of the drying rack. She hated a messy kitchen.

"Can I help you?" When Stella opened the back door, Buddy remained on full alert, fur on the back of his neck pointing straight up. The man stepped carefully around the dog, clutching the folder.

"Miss Davis?" He paused.

"Used to be. Now I'm Mrs. Akpik." She looked her guest up and down and side-to-side. "Who's asking?"

"Uh, uh, I'm Darrell, Darrell Belcher." He fumbled in his inside jacket pocket and handed her a business card. "I'd like to talk to you about an easement for a pipeline that's coming through Monroe County." He held up the file folder for her to see.

Stella wondered if she could handle this fleshy man if she let him in the house and he turned on her. She remembered that her little pistol, the Pink Lady, was in a kitchen drawer behind the silverware tray. "Just reach me those papers through the door." He hesitated. "I can read them myself, Mister."

"I'd like to explain the map to you, Ma'am."

Now she was getting aggravated. "I can read a map, too, Mister."

Chapter 9

He mentally regrouped as he turned up his coat collar against the wind. "Tell me this, do you own the land beyond the red barn west of the road over there?"

Stella thought about that for a bit and asked the question she could not answer herself. "What do you need to know that for?"

"Mountain Top Pipeline needs to buy an easement across the top of that piece of land for the pipeline that's coming through."

Stella perked up. "That 42-inch pipeline that carries natural gas liable to explode at any time?" He sputtered, at a loss for words. Stella enjoyed it and went on with the answer that she thought he might have proposed. "Yes, Sir, I can read newspapers, too. Best you move along."

After a few seconds, he regained words and sputtered, "Well, Ma'am, I wouldn't say it was going to explode. There are safety features that make that practically impossible."

"How much?"

"I'm sorry, how much what?" He found a tissue in spite of the chilly wind and wiped his nose.

"How much money?"

"Oh, it is paid by the foot. Looks like we need about a thousand feet through that field to link the Donegal farm and the Tinney place through your field."

"How much a foot?" Stella stood holding the door in place while he battled the wind to look through his papers.

"Looks like the initial offer is $40 a foot."

It took less than a split second for $40,000 to appear in Stella's mental calculator. "Maybe you better come in and sit a spell and explain this to me."

"I sure appreciate it, Ma'am." The papers were a mess as he stuffed them back into the folder following her through the kitchen door.

Stella sat near the silverware drawer but was too distracted by the money to be concerned by any danger he might pose. She paid close attention as Darrell Belcher, land agent for Mountain Top Pipeline, showed her maps, data sheets, and a contract. She had a lot of questions, some related to actual pipeline construction, dates construction began and ended, and the final destination of the gas being transported, but she saved the most important one for last. "Well, Mr. Belcher, what if I don't want a pipeline coming across my sheep field?"

The land agent, finally warm and comfortable, leaned back in the kitchen chair. "Then, we will condemn the field and pay you the least we can, so we **will** get it anyway. Eminent domain, Mrs. Akpik, enables progress in this country. You should probably take this money; it'll be the best offer." He nodded at the contract, then slid it across the table. Belcher smiled, crossed his arms and watched.

Stella struggled to smile. "So, the access is a hundred feet wide across our pasture, Mountain Top Pipeline workers will have a key to our gate for as long as the pipeline exists, the trench for the pipe is six feet deep, you will cut down all shade trees in the path as soon as possible, and the underground structure is not known, so blasting may occur. Is that all correct?" Misinterpreting her smile, Belcher bobbed his chin up and down, jiggling the folds of flesh underneath.

Stella appeared to be thinking about signing. She even picked up the pen he offered, then laid it back down on the checkered tablecloth. The truth was that she was searching through her extensive vocabulary of curse words to make adjectives to go with his name as she calculated how to get him on his way and stop the proposed pipeline. She decided on a dumb girl defense. "Mr. Belcher, this is all real nice and I do appreciate you explaining it all so well to me, but you need to know that I got married nearly two years ago and I'd like to —"

He interrupted. "Land is in your name only. You can sign without your husband." He picked up the pen and offered it to her. She took it and went so far as to touch it to the signature line as he leaned forward to watch. Then she looked up.

"But, I do have to live with my husband, so I better give him the chance to agree. I am sure he will," she lied, "but you know, he'll feel left out if I don't talk to him about it." She smiled sweetly and offered him the pen back. "Could you leave the contract and the other information so I can show him?"

"Yes, Ma'am." Belcher's face fell registering the fact that it was over for the moment. "And you just call me when I can come by and pick up the contract." He paused. "After you sign it, that is."

"Oh, yes, indeedy, Mr. Belcher. Your number is on your little calling card, isn't it?" She squinted at it, and then raised her glasses to look again. "Yes, Sir, it's right here." Belcher didn't move and Stella felt the growing tension.

"Don't let me keep you any longer. I bet you have several stops to make today."

Chapter 9

Belcher gave up and groaned as he rose, "Yep, I have several of your neighbors to visit. Hey, do you know any of these landowners?" He showed her a list of names and land parcels. She picked out three names and gave the long way around directions to their homes. He was grateful, having bumped up poorly maintained roads for two weeks without a lot of progress. She showed him the door and hurried to call each of the three mountain neighbors to warn them.

Chapter 10

Beauty of the Land

That evening as Stella carried sweet feed to the sheep barn she noticed the sunset as if her glasses prescription had been improved. Brilliant shades of red and pink swept across the sky. The sheep were eager to greet her, as always, or maybe it was the blue coffee can of sweet feed that piqued their interest. By the time she had fed and watered them and visited a minute, telling them about the pipeline invasion, it was getting darker. She locked the barn door and swept the sky with her eyes, but the lines and colors of the sunset were fading.

Chapter 10

Time got away from her as she soaked in the silence; some tree limbs creaks as they rubbed together. She heard the rustle of broom sage in the next field as the wind blew the brown plants all in one direction. She sat on a limestone outcropping and listened to a dog barking far away and caught a whiff of wood smoke drifting up from houses down below. The cold of the rock finally worked through her jeans and she stood. She wondered, as she had dozens of times, how far inside the earth did that particular rock go. Her next puzzle was the ever-changing sinkholes. Made by the collapse of underground cavern roofs, she had read. They appeared, then filled up again, and then reopened. *Funny how the earth changes deep inside, but all that changes on the outside are the sinkholes, well, and all the human damage. Pavement and buildings and chemicals everywhere and now, now a pipeline. Here, on our mountain, in our lifetime, a big ole pipe carrying natural gas right through our sheep field. Coming through yards and creeks and over the steep mountain. What will it do to the way we live?*

She saw the outline of an eagle roosting in the leafless dead tree that was part of the fence line. The bird's shoulders were hunched over and the white feathers looked like a lady's glowing shawl, pulled close in the cold. As she walked down the lane back to the house, she noticed for the first time this season how far down the valley she could see car lights. The trees were bare sticks and she could see all the way to US Route 219. Couldn't hear the trucks and cars but their headlights twinkled all the way to the mountain, probably three miles away as the crow flies. She tried not to imagine the sounds of bulldozers and cranes moving lengths of pipe into the grassy ground.

The stars were out and the moon was rising before she made it back to the house. *It's not late*, she told herself, *the days are just getting shorter.* She looked up at the sky and found the three stars of Orion's belt and drew mental lines to the stars that made up his body and sword. *How small we all are. Every one of those twinkling lights could host millions of living things, just like here on Earth.* She waited a while on the deck while the music of the coyotes started. As much as she hated the killing beasts, especially when the lambs were young, she loved to listen to their yipping. *Having a party tonight, aren't you? Inviting guests from the next ridge, it sounds like.*

Stella finally went inside. "You've been gone a while, been worried about you, you all right?" Jonas was folding the daily paper as he walked through the house.

Stella knew that if he had ventured from the recliner, he was concerned. Her boots thumped as she kicked them off in the hallway and the fragrance of molasses-fueled sheep manure wafted up from the floor. "Sorry to worry you. I'm okay. Just soaking in the beauty of the land tonight." She was slipping on her inside shoes and didn't look up at Jonas, or she would've seen his eyebrows knitted and lowered over his tired brown eyes.

"Stella," he drug out her name, "maybe you better tell me what's going on."

"Aw, I don't know, just feeling change in the air and it kinda unsettles me." She finally straightened up and stretched backward to relieve her back from being bent over frontward for so long.

Jonas wasn't satisfied, but he grunted and acted like he was, then went back to reading the paper. Stella turned the TV on, checked out the news and then a sit-com, then clicked the remote off and started to look for the book she was reading. The land agent's visit had worked her into a stew. It was like hearing that a loved one was dying but you were in the will. That pipeline would just ruin the land. But $40 grand would satisfy Jonas and he could complete the retirement paperwork happily and be home with her.

Stella rubbed her temples, the throbbing that came before a headache was beginning. Jonas shook his head, knowing the signs of Stella's attempts to keep secrets, at least from him. He put down the paper and spoke tenderly, "Out with it, Babe. There is nothing that you and I together can't figure out."

"I think we are lost this time." Her pale blue eyes were red-rimmed and weak, another sign of stress Jonas recognized. "Let me get a Dr. Pepper. C'mon in the kitchen, I have some papers to show you."

Bewildered, he dropped the newspaper behind him in the recliner and followed her to the round oak kitchen table, the setting for many conversations, some of them very difficult. He got a glass from the cupboard as she fumbled opening her can of pop, then sat back down as she poured it and took a long swallow. "Stella, get on with it, you are making me nervous."

"A man came here today, Jonas. He sat right in this chair and he told me that the company he works for wants to buy access to the top sheep pasture."

Jonas brightened, "Sounds like good news to me. What do they want it for?"

Chapter 10

"Oh, it is so not good news at all but I thought it was at first. It is terrible news. A huge natural gas pipeline is coming across Peters Mountain and coming through our land and we can't stop it and what good is the money if we can't even be safe in our own home? Oh, Jonas, I am so hurt and, and ... " she threw the empty pop can towards the trash can across the room, " ... so, so angry." She looked around for something else to throw and reached for the contract Belcher had left, but Jonas took her hand and just held it.

Then they talked themselves through a number of options from moving to Canada (which they later giggled about), to getting a lawyer, to taking the money and getting out of the way. Along about midnight, they agreed that it was too much to absorb in one evening and went to bed. Jonas fell asleep right away but Stella, wrapped spoon-like against his body in his arms, did not. She revisited each undefeatable demon of her past and reviewed how she overcame every one of them. By the time little Napoleon, the banty rooster, began crowing, she was strengthened by her own history. She finally went to sleep with Jonas's words in her heart: *You are a survivor. There is nothing we can't figure out together.*

Chapter 11

Back to the Beach – Sea View Nursing Home

"What do you think about Reverend Jonathan?" a tiny, hunched-over woman whispered to her friends as she used the heel of her arthritic hands to scoot her cards to the table's edge and pick them up between two fingers.

"Oh, he is a dear." Margaret spread the cards smoothly in her hand like a fan.

"I think he's hot." Naomi spoke again, seriously.

"Naomi, keep your bloomers on, you think anyone under seventy-five in pants is hot." Margaret spoke and they all

Chapter 11

laughed. She was the undisputed leader of the gaggle of elderly women seated around the card table in the sunroom. They tried to keep their laughter down. They'd been chastised by the staff when their card games got too loud and were trying to stay out of trouble, at least for the time being.

Sometimes they just had had enough of being told when and what they could do and rebelled. Like the time the supervisor banished a sassy Margaret back to her room. Alone in her room and angry, she promptly left a puddle of urine on the floor just inside the door so the next staff member to enter slid and fell. "Bet they didn't see that coming," she had whispered the next day. "I told them I didn't do it, maybe the FBI could run a DNA test to see who did." The other women were awed by her pluck. Most of the residents of Sea View were cowed down by illness and fear. Margaret was not.

The rummy game continued. The cluster of women around the table joked and made fun of one another as they struggled with holding and playing their cards. Other residents sat behind the first row and helped those playing the game, either by reaching their cards to them or helping them to select a card to play or calculating the score when someone declared "Rummy." Players would rotate in and out. A fringe of canes and walkers circled the group. They'd play after lunch until someone needed a nap. The house rule was that if you dozed off at the table, you lost your turn. Margaret had made the rule and ran the game like a pro. She also had several decks of cards. Once before, a staff member confiscated their cards when they wouldn't be quiet and Margaret had simply pulled another deck from her purse. She knew they were looking for her six other decks, so she had them hidden all over the facility, like Easter eggs. She was also on the lookout for the deck that had been taken. "Good clean fun – like hide and seek," she said.

In fact, in all things, they turned to Margaret for guidance. There was something intangible about her that people liked. Maybe it was her quick pixie smile, her thoughtful gaze, the fact that she was a good listener or that she had no time for nonsense or drama. Her words were honest and blunt, but always spoken with kindness and often with dry humor. She said she was 74 years old, but seemed younger since she was in such good physical and mental shape. Her silver hair was cut short and had been for as long as she had been a resident there. She did not wear the gowns and robes popular with many; instead she put on a touch of makeup and not so subtle jewelry every day, along with outdoor clothing and shoes. Often, she wore colorful jogging suits, not that she ever jogged these days. Some of the residents speculated that she had no family and no place to go because she so seldom had visitors. She said that she had chosen this facility at Myrtle Beach in hopes that the grandkids would want to come to the beach to see her. So far, it wasn't working, but she was willing to give it time. For now, the "girls" were her family.

Today's card game was lively. Reverend Jonathan Wesley, the new man in their lives, had stirred them up. "He's probably married with ten grandchildren," Rosie added to the speculations and cut her eyes coyly.

"I heard he was single," Naomi added.

"Where did you hear that?" Margaret sliced and diced rumors often.

"Well, he told me so hisself." Naomi crossed her crippled hands in her lap and nodded her head once to put the final punctuation on her validation.

"Anybody here ever heard of a married man that lied?" Margaret spoke but kept on collecting the cards while the women shared examples of just that situation with one another.

Naomi was resolute and raised her voice above the chatting, "If Reverend Jonathan says it, I believe it."

Margaret glanced at the desk, "Oh, no, ladies, here comes the nurse. Pipe down." Voices immediately stilled. Only the slap of cards against each other as they were expertly shuffled could be heard when Nurse Danvers stepped up to the table.

"Getting a little rowdy over here, ladies. Everything okay?"

The quiet must have awakened Rosemary in the wheelchair. She replied, "We are fine, just fine. Now sit down and do your work." Rosemary had been an elementary teacher for 45 years and had some phrases embedded in her memory that came out especially when she was sleepy. She was on autopilot, her friends realized. Nurse Danvers didn't take offense at Rosemary, but she gave the rest of the group what they called her evil eye. Before Margaret, it was enough to send them to their rooms, but now they just looked away. "Not meeting her eyes destroys her power," was Margaret's opinion.

"Just one more game and we'll break for a nap," Margaret countered the evil eye without looking up, giving the nurse in charge a chance to save face.

"Meds at two o'clock, I'll see you all in your rooms." She walked away and the whispering began.

"I don't like the way she announces meds, like it's a threat."

"We pay her salary, she's got no right to boss us."

"It is not nice to bully." Rosemary was startled awake by the voices, spoke, then dozed off again.

"Can someone do my nails before Reverend Jonathan comes this afternoon?" Naomi looked around her circle of friends, covering one twisted hand with the other. Her words started another round of tittering.

Teeny spoke up, "Look at this bunch, Naomi, not a steady hand among them. Me either for that matter, but I'll try. Do you have the polish and some remover to clean up the mess?"

Naomi beamed. "Yes, I have the pads not the liquid, but I like them better. Let's go now?" Teeny nodded and Naomi announced her vacancy at the table. She pushed on her chair to get up and trundled off with Teeny to her room. The women chuckled and continued to play, but Margaret sensed what the others were feeling: Naomi was going to get her feelings hurt.

Chapter 12

Follow the Money

If Jonathan Wesley knew that he had the nursing home residents gabbing about him, the prideful male within would be disgusted and the scheming part of him would be thrilled. At this point, he was 99% schemer, thinking only of the big score, which he did all day, from the decisions about what he wore to the words he said to the hours he spent researching the possibilities.

He'd opened the mail addressed to Naomi Waterman and learned that she had a savings account of nearly a hundred thousand dollars and a checking account with a hefty monthly income and regular automatic payments to Sea View. He had photocopied the account statements before resealing them inside their envelopes. He returned them to the bundle of mail the next day. There were questions to be answered, though. Was there more? Land? Stocks? Where was her family? Did she have a friend or family member who had been given power of attorney? He aimed to get answers soon. Then he would plan his next move.

First, he needed to have total access to Naomi's mail. He delivered it five days a week, but he wasn't there on Saturdays and feared he might miss something important. When he spoke to her the next day, he encouraged her to keep her mail in one place so he could leave it there if she was not in her room when the mail came.

"Why, Reverend Wesley, I look forward to seeing you every day. I make it a point to be here when you stop by." And she did, with bright lipstick and rosy circles of powdered rouge, both often misapplied. The preacher cringed at the lipstick on her teeth and unevenly blushing cheeks. But he sensed her weaknesses and took in her crippled hands and body and the loneliness of her existence with delight. He decided to move forward.

"I'm tired today, Mrs. Waterman, may I sit and visit with you a while?"

"Oh, yes, there's a chair, just p-p-pull it over here." She stuttered with excitement. "And do call me N-Naomi." She beamed as he moved an upholstered chair over beside her rocking chair.

"Well, Naomi, I didn't want to take liberties, but are you 'Mrs.' or 'Miss?' Is there a Mr. Waterman?" he asked her.

"Oh, my, yes, there **was** a Mr. Waterman." Naomi giggled as Jonathan's stomach dropped. "He was my husband and he's been d-d-dead for many years."

Trying hard to conceal his grin, Jonathan expressed his sorrow for her loss, which she nodded away. Boldly, she asked, "How about you, Reverend, are you married?"

"No, Naomi, my wife passed many years ago." He was again able to disguise his true thought: *that bitch I left a lifetime ago is probably still looking for me.*

At the same instant, Naomi thought, *now I have made the lie I told the girls the other day the truth.*

The two chatted a bit longer about the weather and her favorite hymns. He promised to sing one of them for her that afternoon. They were both delighted as they replayed their conversation over and over mentally in the following days.

* * * * *

Mail started piling up in the basket on Naomi's dresser. She had agreed that Reverend Wesley would leave it there for her to look at later. So far, no Saturday letters had come. There were bank statements and tax tickets and one life insurance invoice, paid by an automatic withdrawal from her checking account. There was only one item of personal correspondence, a Thanksgiving card with a scrawled signature, "Love, Penny."

It made the preacher nervous. *Who in the world is Penny?* He was also worried that Naomi didn't seem interested in her mail, so he took the next, carefully planned, step.

During his regular visit, he commented, "Naomi, do you need some help with your mail, it is just lying there. I would be happy to help." Quickly he added, "That is, if you need any help."

Realizing the golden opportunity to spend more time with her "beau" as she now thought of him, she jumped at the chance. Batting her eyes, she unknowingly did a Scarlet O'Hara impression, "Why, Jonathan, I'd just love your help. All those numbers and papers to sign just overwhelm poor little me."

And thus, the door was opened for Jonathan Wesley to explore the life and business of Ms. Naomi Waterman, a wealthy, elderly, and unmarried woman. He congratulated himself each day for his wise choice as he moved in for the crowning moment: to be allowed legal access. Now, he wanted to have power of attorney status. Naomi had a goal herself; she wanted more intimate physical contact and had asked him to hold her hand while they talked.

He muttered, "Of course, My Dear," and took her hand in his, repulsed at the stiff claw that trembled at his touch. She gently rubbed his hands and found the missing joint on a finger. "What happened to your finger?" She was shy about asking and stared at the end of the finger while she waited for his answer.

"High school shop class." He chuckled. "I learned to be more careful."

"You poor dear." She raised it to her lips like a mother kissing a boo-boo. Jonathan squeezed her hand in response.

The next day, she asked him to touch her face and he obliged, cupping his hand around the jawline of her little cheek. He thought the time was right to pop the question: his request to have power of attorney. "Naomi, my dear ..."

With eyes closed, she sighed, "Don't say a word, Jonathan, just let me enjoy the warmth of your hand." She opened her eyes and smiled gratefully at him. The moment passed and he hurried out to continue delivering mail to the residents.

This is getting out of hand, he laughed to himself, but he knew he had done much worse for less money. *This could be a fortune.*

* * * * *

Chapter 12

Jonathan assumed that the budding relationship was a secret only he and Naomi shared. Little did he know that his daily visits alerted Naomi's friends. They knew all about his time with her.

Card games buzzed with questions. "What do you suppose he's after?" posed one of the women.

"Maybe he's trying to sell her something."

"Oh, come on, he's after her money."

"Does she even have any money?"

"Shhh, here she comes." The women changed the subject, talking about an outing that was planned for the next Tuesday: a trip to the mall's beauty shop. They had a beautician at Sea View who came in a couple of days a month, but it just wasn't the same as going to a shop and getting a manicure or pedicure and a hair styling. Some of the ladies hoped to walk a lap around the mall just to window shop. At any rate, it would take most of the afternoon.

"Name your game, ladies." Margaret offered a variety of card games and was willing to teach novices any of them, but the favorite was Rummy. She asked every day, however, just in case. She understood that as much as they all hated the loss of freedom they had, they also liked consistency.

Naomi spoke up, "How about poker today?" Heads swiveled to look at her.

"Feeling lucky?" Margaret asked. The women couldn't look away.

Naomi brightened, "I am feeling **blessed**," she announced. "I have a new friend."

"Do tell." Margaret had frozen, the deck of cards in her hand.

"Well, he is very nice and we talk and I think he wants to spend more time with me." She covered her mouth with her misshapen hand as if she had said a bad word or as if she was bragging improperly. Her eyes sparkled as she looked around the table, appearing very much like a teenage girl experiencing puppy love.

"Boys are trouble." Rosemary seemed very sure of this fact.

"Who is it?"

"Tell us about him."

Naomi couldn't resist. "It's Jonathan. Reverend Wesley." She squealed a little saying his name.

The women feigned surprise. "Well, you little scamp. Found a man right under our nose." Teeny was pleased for her friend.

They looked at one another. The elephant at the card table hovered there: *Who was going to tell her about the very likely possibility that he was using her?* Eyes made their way to Margaret.

Margaret cleared her throat and put on a happy face. "Naomi, we are so happy for you. Have you introduced him to anyone in your family? The holidays are coming and it would be a good time."

"I'll have to ask Jonathan if he has time. He is very busy, you know, with his church and all."

"Not very busy. He's here every day, all day, ev—." The speaker stopped abruptly as a well-placed kick hit her shin under the table.

The group had already racked their brains to come up with someone they should alert about this situation and had not remembered any visitors or a single name that Naomi had mentioned. "Who will come to see you at Christmas time?" Margaret probed gently.

"Penny might come." Naomi was thoughtful. "Penny. I could let him know."

Looks were exchanged and the majority of the women knew that they must find out who Penny was. That, and the clear directive that Naomi was to enjoy her happiness as long as she could, but everyone was on high alert to protect her if or when Reverend Wesley misbehaved.

Chapter 13

Pondering the Pipeline

"Well, Stella, you've got to poison your pick. Either you choose the lump sum of cash and open the gate for the pipeline to come through the sheep field, or we close that gate by fighting the proposed route tail and nooth." Jonas and Stella had discussed their options day and night until he was tired of it. They were on the way to church in the truck when the discussion erupted again.

"It's 'pick your poison' and 'tooth and nail,' or do you do that just to aggravate me?" Stella wasn't feeling too agreeable. She hated to pass up the money, but she also hated to lose control of her land.

"Okay, just imagine you have made one of the choices for a day," Jonas suggested calmly, "and see how it feels."

Stella pondered that quietly until they pulled into the church parking lot. As she stepped down from the passenger seat, she decided to pretend that she had sold out. She informed Jonas and then began spending the money. "First thing I'd do is get this parking lot paved. People get tired of wearing clean shoes to church and going into worship with muddy feet." Jonas laughed and figured that would take a lot of the imaginary $40,000, but he kept his thoughts to himself.

Church attendance was sparse, but Stella enjoyed the service even if there weren't many there to visit with. The new preacher was working out just fine; he had a good clear voice and was big on scripture. *Hard to go wrong when you preach the scripture*, Stella thought. *Preacher Booth was a good one, but he wasn't sure that I didn't take that benefit dinner money year before last and he hired Timmy Lee to fund-raise. Surely that was the dumbest thing he ever did. Best I get over that, it's been long enough past.* Stella was deep in thought when the offering plate was passed to her and she put her regular check in it. "Just think," she whispered to Jonas, "I could write a check for a hundred dollars every week with that pipeline money." He nodded and calculated it would all be spent within two hours if she ever got that money for real.

On the way home, Jonas stopped in sight of the sheep barn and the fattened ewes in the field and asked, "In your pretend game, how do you see the heavy equipment getting to the top field to dig the trench?"

"Oh, the sections of pipe and the equipment travel the route of the pipeline. They don't have to travel on our little winding roads. I asked Mr. Belcher."

"What if they skip around and need to get to a section of route that is beyond a section with a delay?" Jonas was familiar with pipeline construction from the oil fields of Alaska and Louisiana.

Stella looked toward the distant field. "I figured that they would start at one end and go to the other end, all in order. Mr. Belcher didn't say anything about skipping a section."

"Lots of things can cause one section to be delayed. Migratory songbirds can nest at certain times of the year and the trees can't be cut down. Blasting may go haywire. Equipment breaks down. Legal problems can prevent access for months. A steep section might have a rockslide or even a mudslide if the weather turns wet. You can never tell." He patted her leg. "But you'll have the big money."

Stella pretended the rest of that day that she had money to spend. She thumbed through seed catalogs and the Premier farm supply catalog and turned back the corners of pages that showed items she wanted. At the top of her list was a solar-powered automatic chicken coop door. At only $300, it would give her the ability to stay out late and sleep late without worrying about putting the chickens up. She closed the catalog with a happy sigh and decided to go for a walk. Buddy was ready to go, getting feeble, but still dancing in circles as Stella grabbed a jacket.

"You want company?" Jonas had kept an eye on her while he piddled around the house. He'd built a fire in the fireplace insert and had watched some parts of college football games, then studied the Sunday paper while she shopped the catalogs. He had an idea where she was going.

"No, I'll take Buddy with me. I am still pretending that we give access to the pipeline and I am going to go up to the top field and pretend to say goodbye."

"Figured you needed to take a look. Take the map so you can see exactly where the pipe will be."

"Okay." She rummaged around through the opened mail and found the map. "Won't be gone long."

"Be careful, Hon." The sound of the kitchen door closing was his only answer. *Stella is no more going to sell her land than I am going to sprout wings and fly. She'd more likely give it to somebody than make money from a pipeline that only helps line corporate wallets.* Satisfied, he sat in thought a few seconds, then chuckled again as he opened the paper back up to read and spoke aloud. "Now, how she's gonna stop the blasted pipeline once she decides it's not for her, I do not know."

Stella traipsed sadly all around the field, noticed that there were some surveyor ribbons on the fence and figured that's where the pipe would come through. While Stella was pacing off the distance between fences, Buddy sniffed a rabbit out of a briar patch; both animals were surprised. Buddy chased it down into the valley, yelping after he lost it.

The dog trotted back, tongue lolling out within a few minutes, giving Stella time to check out the ancient oak trees that would have to be cut down. She tried to measure them, but they were all so big her arms wouldn't even go halfway around them. She left her arms up and talked to the tree. "Yes, Sir, this is a hug. I love you, big oak tree. I love all the shade that you've made for cattle and sheep and all the acorns you've dropped for the deer. And I don't think I can bear to have you cut down, even for a big pile of money." The wind cut through her jacket on the way back and chilled her to the bone. She had little to say and went to bed early so she could end the day and stop pretending she had sold out.

On Monday, her friend Tisha called and wanted to know if she was up for an evening out. "Let's drive down to Fancy Gap. I need to get some ribbons for Christmas wreaths and flowers for arrangements. Then we can eat in that place that used to be a gas station that's fixed up with all the car stuff, like light fixtures made of license plates and checkered flags for curtains. Crankshaft Café or something like that. Eliza'll go if you'll go," Tisha tried to tempt her.

"What kind of food do they serve?" Stella was glad to get out of the house, but she liked to know what to expect.

Chapter 13

"Well, it's not what you'd call fine dining, but it's priced right and the food is good. Breakfast all day and all kinds of burgers and hot dogs and pickle fries. I haven't had them but people say they are good." Tisha paused to get a breath. "The people working there look clean and the restaurant is real cute and eat off the floor clean. C'mon, let's go. Meet me after school tomorrow at the ATM machine lot, about 5:00?"

"Yeah, I'll go." Stella let a little excitement creep into her voice.

"I'll leave a pot of beans on for Jonas," and she thought, *he could practice making his very own cornbread for supper.*

Chapter 14

Tales of the Pipeline

Stella met Jonas at the door when he got home from work to tell him that she was going out shopping with Tisha and Eliza within the hour and that there were warm beans in the crock-pot, and he could make his own cornbread. He roared with laughter. She threw a little box of Spiffy mix at him and went upstairs to put up her hair, giggling a little herself. He followed her to the bathroom and stood behind her looking in the mirror, put his arms around her waist, then slipped them under her sweater and massaged her warm skin, then unhooked her bra.

Chapter 14

She squealed, "Now stop it, Jonas. I am going out to shop and eat and I need to be in Peterstown in an hour, so I need to leave in 35 minutes."

"So," he said kissing her neck and sliding his gentle hands around to her front, "what could we do for the next 25 minutes?" She waved her brush at him so he could see it in the mirror, but it was a weak attack. "Could be done in 20 minutes if everything goes just right," he whispered.

And she caved. Everything did go just right and very soon she scampered down the hallway wearing only socks to the bathroom to shower. Afterwards, she gathered up her underclothes and sweater and jeans from the trail of clothing between the bathroom and the bed. When she got to the bedroom to dress, Jonas was propped up on one elbow, grinning from ear to ear. "All that built up tension over the pipeline and my retirement. It's not healthy. Good thing I am here to help you with that." She threw a pillow at him and scurried into her clothes, pulled her hair into a ponytail and pinned it up.

"That's a poor excuse for a hairdo," she said into the dresser mirror, "but it will have to do. And you, you, Sir," she pointed her hairbrush at him. "You are a distraction." Then she went to the bed and held his face in her hands and kissed him. "I do love you, Jonas Akpik, and all the 'healing' you do for me. But, I gotta go." She ran down the stairs in high spirits trying to still get to town by five o'clock.

By the time she pulled into the ATM parking lot, Stella was feeling great. She threw herself into the front seat of Tisha's new SUV and they had to wait only a minute more for Eliza's arrival. The three had been friends for years at work and at home. Together, they had faced and survived illnesses, courtships, and financial woes. On this day, by the time they hit the Virginia state line, all the small talk was dispensed with and the conversation turned to the main concern of each woman. For Stella, the pipeline decision, for Tisha, her youngest son moving out, and for Eliza, the care of her father.

Halfway to Fancy Gap, Tisha was comforted that their baby boy Eddie was only moving five miles away and would be living on her route to work so she could keep an eye on him. In another 20 miles, Eliza had the names and numbers of several home care workers who free-lanced after hours and would know other people who could sit with her dad, and the name of a respite care facility where he would likely qualify for free care a few days a month. She also explained that he didn't need the help yet, he was perking right along, but she wanted to have a plan for the coming years. They promised to discuss the pipeline pros and cons over supper at the Crankshaft Café.

"Can't wait to see those walls of ribbons and rooms of silk flowers at the Fancy Gap Outlet." Tisha had a side business of flower arrangements and wreaths during the holidays to supplement her school clerk's salary, and this trip to the outlet was a business investment.

"What are you making money for? I just love to watch you set goals and make them happen." Stella didn't mind being nosy with her friends.

"Just Christmas gifts for the family this year. I want to get our new daughter-in-law some copper-bottom pans for one thing, and something nice for Tom, and help Jeb with his last semester of graduate school fees."

Eliza asked, "Does she not know how to cook yet? Maybe you should get her a cookbook instead of pans."

"Shoot, the both of them have burned up every single pan they got as wedding gifts and you all know how many gifts they got."

After filling the back of the SUV with ribbons and flowers bought at the rustic outlet, they headed up the road to the car-themed restaurant. It was just as Tisha had described, the floor like a checkered flag, silver wall panels made of the same metal as truck bed liners, and tool boxes and every item on the menu named for cars. They each ordered a different sandwich, a Cadillac, a Mustang, and a Bellaire, plus a big order of pickle fries to share.

While they waited, the talk turned to the pipeline. "The guy that owns that hunting cabin, the one your brother hid out in, his land is right in the path of the pipeline. They offered him $56,000 for it." Tisha spoke with authority. "Then he took that chubby little land agent out and wined and dined him ..."

"Mostly wined, I heard," Eliza added.

"Well, yes, they were drunk as hoot owls, but he came home with an offer of $96,000. He signed the next day."

"Wow." Stella was impressed.

"But wait, it was not all good news. He got a lot of that money to cover damages and there hasn't been any damages yet so he had to pay taxes for last year on the money. Get this, at 41%."

Chapter 14

"Well then, he'll just have to pay it." Eliza thought in black and white.

Tisha continued, "But he can't. The fool spent all the money already!" Their order was delivered about then. The women wiped meat juices off their chins and laughed and generally had a very pleasant meal, when a man came over and offered to buy their dinner if they'd talk with him a while.

Tisha glanced at her friends, saw no panic or strong feelings, and took charge. "Honey, you just sit down in the booth with us. We'll talk your leg off. You don't need to buy us any dinner." Eliza excused herself and went to talk to the waitress in hopes of finding out about the man.

"Oh, no. I'll get him to leave. His name is Howard and he is just lonely."

"No, that won't be necessary. I was just checking on his story."

The waitress continued while refilling salt and pepper shakers at the counter, "The owner used to be friends with his son, so he lets him hang out here. He's harmless, but if you want him moved, I can do it."

Eliza rejoined the group who were finishing up. They bid Howard goodbye and Tisha caught her up in the car. "Howard has invited us down in the spring to hunt 'sang' with him. Says he knows all the best ginseng places."

"Did you know him before tonight?" Eliza attempted to make his visit logical.

"Did not know him from Adam's house cat." Tisha and Stella laughed as they re-entered the interstate, talking about other times they had attracted crazy people. Thoughts of Timmy Lee shadowed her mind and she was subdued for a while. *Was he also clinging to strange people in restaurants to have someone to talk to?*

The women told pipeline tales all the way home. Eliza had heard that the pipeline was 300 miles long and 90% of the needed easements in northern WV had been signed over; but in little Summers and Monroe Counties, only 60% of landowners had agreed to the terms Mountain Top had proposed.

"Why are more people holding out in Monroe County?" Stella wondered out loud.

"Because our families have worked hard to keep their land. Some farmers are seventh generation on the same plot of land. Money doesn't count much against ties like that." Eliza continued, "People here write stories about the land, they sing songs about the mountains, the culture of mountain life is almost gone anyway and losing land to a stinking pipeline is another nail in the coffin of our way of life."

Tisha turned down the radio to speak seriously. "Maybe ANY way of life. If those things leak, they can explode and there are fireballs and the ground shakes. The one through MoCo goes close to our high school and the biggest nursing home. Isn't that great planning?"

They all thought about that for a moment, then Tisha remembered another tragedy. "Then those poor fellows in Illinois got a tractor stuck and went to get another tractor to pull it out, hit the pipe and ka-boom! A father and son were killed in the explosion."

"And the water, Tish, don't forget that – we have pristine spring water feeding the water system for both ends of the county, and heaven only knows what will happen underground when they start blasting."

Stella listened to every word and grew quiet on the way home. Her own decision was made, but how could she protect others from the dangers that Mountain Top Pipeline posed?

Chapter 15

Naomi's Romance

Naomi was basking in the warmth of her new friendship. She let the beautician experiment with a new hair color that showed less bluish tint at the roots and spent too much money ordering a new perfume: Rhianna's "Kiss," guaranteed to "leave a lasting impression."

She spent more time grooming and reading *True Confessions* and romance novels and less time with her friends at the home.

Reverend Wesley noticed her reading materials in a rack near her rocking chair and did a mental eye roll. *Surely, she isn't considering actual sex,* he hoped. But every visit, she shyly requested more touching, for him to rub her back or massage her shoulders. *I've got to head this off soon,* he realized.

* * * * *

Unbeknownst to Naomi and Jonathan, the girls were watching the couple's every move. In the room across the hall from hers, there was a resident in a wheelchair whose assignment was to time exactly when Jonathan went into the room with the mail and exactly when he came out. Another woman figured up the times spent alone together. Margaret got the notes and saw that in the three weeks they'd been watching, the time had increased from under five minutes up to a consistent  fifteen-minute time period daily. Another lady had noticed that his time with other residents had grown shorter, and was miffed. Naomi wasn't the only woman that had set her cap for

Jonathan, but now he barely noticed the others, dashing in and leaving the mail quickly.

As Christmas approached, the nursing home seemed cheerful with decorations and the hallways more chaotic with more visitors and new faces. Margaret made it a point to sit with Naomi at lunch during the festive times and managed to insert a question into the conversation, "Do you expect Penny to visit during the holidays?" Naomi laid her fork down and glared at Margaret.

"How do you know about Penny? What business is that of yours?"

"Why, Honey, you told me about him. Remember when I asked if you were going to introduce your gentleman friend to your family? You mentioned Penny."

"Harrumph. Penny is busy." Naomi didn't remember mentioning Penny and was aggravated. She resumed eating, carefully because of her twisted fingers. She took her time and lined the fork up with the food, then balanced it cautiously on the time-consuming trek to her mouth. And that was all Margaret learned, but she did notice that Naomi's fingers had loosened up and worked normally when she was angry.

* * * * *

Jonathan carefully chose the time to make his "love" known. It had to be a time that Naomi would feel romantic and daring. Late Christmas Eve after his Christmas carol sing-a-long seemed to be a good time, and he was confident he could smooth away any doubts with his words. He had always been able to talk his way through any rough edges.

Naomi actually set up his visit. "When will I see you again?" she whispered after the Christmas caroling.

"I'll stop by your room late, at bedtime. I have a special gift for you." He smiled and patted her on the shoulder and gave it a little squeeze. He had to get his act together, to set up the "gift-giving" just right to make it suffice for ownership and the legal rights that he was determined to win. He had to make a trip to Wal-Mart and make several small purchases, then run home to complete the charade before heading back to Naomi's room.

She was light-headed with happiness, not sure what was coming but certain that it involved a gift for her, and a wonderful one if it was from Jonathan. She hoped that he would like her gift to him, an ornate leather-bound Bible.

He returned to Sea View late for nursing home residents, about ten o'clock, and entered through the kitchen where no one was on duty. The halls were quiet and he slipped into her room where she awaited him in a pink Chantilly lace gown worn under a matching pink satin kimono. All this in a cloud of Rhianna's latest perfume.

"Ah, you are lovely tonight." Jonathan tried to focus on the shadows of the dimly lit room. "Merry Christmas, Darling."

Naomi giggled as she thanked him. Childishly, she couldn't wait to see his reaction to her gift. "Let me go first," she begged.

"Sure, Honey, whatever you want."

"Look up there, in the closet shelf." She pointed with her hand. "It's wrapped especially for you." He resented having to spend time on pretending to like her gift, but saw her level of excitement and knew there was no way out.

"What could it be?" He shook the box and guessed, "Candy? A shirt?" Naomi was clapping her hands together with anticipation.

"No, no. Open it and see." He paused before he carefully slid a finger under the taped paper, smiling at her. "Oh, hurry, Jonathan, I just can't wait."

The paper fell away and he hesitated again before opening the cardboard box, extending the sweet pain of her anticipation. "Why, a Bible!" He touched the cover longingly then hugged her and kissed her forehead. She was overcome with emotion.

"Now, it's my turn." His voice trembled a bit, impressing even himself with its sincerity. "I don't have a gift as grand as yours, but my sentiment is every bit as fine. I want to commit my life to you, Naomi."

Her eyes widened. "But I know there are those against us, some because of our small age difference and some for other reasons." He began to unbutton his red dress shirt. "So, I want to keep this private, just between you and me." Naomi nodded, without a clue of what was to come. He slid his shirt back over one tanned shoulder and there was a small tattoo, a heart encircling the letters NW. She gasped.

"That's me!"

"Yes, Naomi, I am making a commitment to serve you symbolized by this outward symbol of my devotion and dedication to you." His voice had taken on that of a preacher during a ritual. He moved forward so that she could see it, but not close enough to touch. "It's still sore," he explained.

Chapter 15

"Did it hurt much to get that done?"

"Not enough to stop me. Now, the question is, would you be willing to make the same commitment to me?"

Naomi answered by wriggling her shoulder free of the kimono and pushing the strap of her gown aside. "Yes, my love."

Jonathan shook his head thinking, *this is just too easy.* "It will hurt for a while, you understand, and we should wait for a few days to do the initials so you are not too uncomfortable." He proceeded to spout scriptures of strength and bits of wedding ceremonies as he heated the tiny metal heart-shaped canapé cutter with a cigarette lighter. "For the husband is the head of the wife, saith the Lord. Naomi, do you surrender yourself to me?"

"Yes," she murmured, and he pressed the metal heart on the tender flesh above her breast.

"Then, don't you make a sound." She nodded as tears flowed from her tiny red-rimmed eyes. He pressed harder than he needed to and her skin smoked but she didn't cry out. *Ain't love grand,* he thought. He realized that she had fainted, so he redid the heart while she was unconscious to be sure that it was complete. *Maybe I should do the initials, too,* Jonathan wondered, but she had begun whimpering as she came around and he put the lighter and heart away and buttoned up his shirt. He adjusted her gown and pulled the kimono back in place while he thanked her and reminded her that they were now one before God and it was their secret. He disappeared into the Christmas Eve silence without looking back, filled with the sense of having made a giant step towards his goal. By the time he remembered the Bible she had given him, it was Christmas Day.

Chapter 16

Prepping for MTP

During the Christmas holidays, Jonas decided to reject the early retirement deal. He signed on for another six months, partly because Ben McDaniel had talked him into it and partly because he had a few things he wanted to finish in his department. That gave him a chance to save a little more money, to draw a little more pension, and to get more comfortable with the whole retirement thing. Stella didn't mind. She was busy.

Stella had a new lifestyle. She studied constantly. By the time the New Year rolled around, she'd read hundreds of pages of an environmental impact statement. She had studied topographical maps that showed the exact terrain of the proposed pipeline route, and the in-house engineering protocol for never before navigated steep grades. She filed away all the deadlines for construction and all the negotiable provisions in an easement contract. She sorted court cases involving eminent domain and those based on the environment. She read news articles about recent pipeline protests and watched videos of protests. Previous pipeline construction complaints and difficulties filled several file folders.

Then she started researching lawyers. The list of easement attorneys for the eastern United States was short. Stella compared styles and win-loss records and shortened it further. She spoke to her top three choices by phone, then added three more from the western United States and phoned them. Finally, she hired one: Darrin Lawless from Hallelujah, West Virginia, who was willing to work for half the amount other attorneys had wanted. MTP raised their offer but not by

Chapter 16

much. Stella devoted a great deal of time before she "picked her poison" and knew that keeping an unwanted natural gas pipeline off her land would require stopping construction on the entire 303.5 miles of the proposed line.

For her, it all boiled down to the fact that it was **her** thousand feet of land and she didn't want a pipeline running through it. Eminent domain required a greater public or civic good which she believed had not been met, as no one along the line got to use the gas and the projected profit went back to Mountain Top Pipeline.

Stella met with "Friends of the Mountain," an anti-pipeline political action group and every other fund-raising activist meeting that crossed her very busy email account. She folded letters and baked pies and protested survey companies until Jonas told her, "You might as well have a 9-9 job." She just laughed, did her accounting job during the day and fought the pipeline most evenings.

February came with spring-like weather and baby lambs. Blue skies calmed her and she almost felt that the pipeline shadow was lifting. Almost. A federal judge had ruled that trees couldn't be cut down until the migratory songbird nests had been built and used, so construction would have to wait until at least June, and by then the endangered bats would be out of caves and roosting in those same trees, so it would be November before trees could be touched. That gave the land along the pipeline route a little more time. She had almost relaxed about the whole project. Almost.

Jonas begged her to try a change of scenery. She had been too quiet with her nose in a book or near a computer screen for too long. "Tisha and Eliza are going to Dollywood. You know they'd love to have you along."

"It just isn't my thing," Stella explained. "To ride four hours cramped up in a car to sleep in a strange bed with strange noises all around." Stella shook her head. "I've still got some work to do here."

"Lordy, Woman, what else is there to do?" Jonas couldn't even imagine any phase of the project that Stella hadn't tackled.

"Well, I've got a list of land owners in Monroe County that haven't given permission for construction yet. I believe they should know how much I personally appreciate every one. I want to visit and support those owners that are holding out."

Jonas knew that there was no changing her mind. As she visited in old farmhouses around kitchen tables, she reported back to him the peace and tranquility in those old homes. "Mrs. McDaniel taught me that anything organic, that is everything that's ever been alive, has the power to absorb emotion. These old wooden boards and siding, most of them hewn by hand about a hundred years ago are organic. They hold powerful positive vibes, Jonas."

Jonas struggled to understand why people were not signing away their land. He couldn't believe Monroe County farm families were so well off that they would turn down the amount of money that was being offered. "Do they not need the money?"

"It's not that at all. Sure, they could use money to get braces for little Susie and a new tractor tire and money for school, same as everybody else in this country. But not at the expense of their land. Sometimes, the land in question goes back six or seven generations. Seven generations, Jonas. That goes back to Scotland and Ireland and England. Some people have never lived anywhere else but their piece of land." Stella turned back to her list and sighed. "What will happen next, when people don't sell, is that MTP will file lawsuits to condemn the land. Then, they can pay people less."

"Then, what? You are pretty much alone in this fight." Jonas was familiar with oil and gas laws, the unfairness common people were facing. He also knew the corporate greed and corruption was ever present in areas rich in natural resources. The land in West Virginia had already been raped and pillaged for coal by the mining industry, and the railroads that transported it during the boom years.

"Things will start happening then," Stella smiled in a devilish way that got Jonas's attention. He did a double take.

"Stella, what are you thinking? You better not be bothering any vehicles or equipment." She continued to smile. "I mean it."

"You remember hearing about that army plane that crashed in Lindside in the 1970s?"

"Yeah."

"You remember that the pilots ejected just before the crash?"

"Yeah."

"And what did people think when those fly-boys came dragging a parachute behind them, bruised and scratched, knocking on the front door?"

"Well, they didn't believe them."

Chapter 16

"Why not? There was a burning airplane sticking into the mountain without a sign of a pilot. The men were both in uniform and both said they were pilots."

"One old farmer was so surprised that he didn't trust his own eyes."

"How about the other one?"

"I don't know why, Stella, but he didn't believe it either." Jonas was bewildered.

"How many pipelines have ever gone through here?"

"None, I reckon."

"That is correct, 'bout the same number of Army planes that ever crashed in Lindside before the 70s. After that crash it got real, people drug the porch chairs out on the front yard and watched for planes to hit. Now, they knew it could happen. They were ready." She crossed her arms as if that answered it all.

"What are you saying, Stella?"

"I'm saying that nobody has ever dug a hole deep enough and long enough to contain pipes this big on Peters Mountain, and if this outfit really ever breaks ground, then we are all gonna be out in the yard seeing what they might do next. And we won't trust the next bunch of propaganda because the first deals will be shown up for the lies they are."

She twirled a piece of her hair around a finger then tucked the curl inside a bobby pin holding her topknot. "Then, Jonas, the fight will be on. And I won't have to do anything but watch. Enough seeds will have been planted to have a fine harvest. At least, I hope so."

Chapter 17

J. W.

"Naomi, are you in or not?" The nursing home card games continued throughout the winter months but Naomi didn't always play. She spent a lot of time in her room with her catalogs, ordering clothing and cosmetics. The right Reverend Jonathan Wesley had completed his branding on her chest. She now had a cursive J. and W. in her burnt-on heart. The brand had assumed the power of a marriage license in her mind and she continued to pursue "her" Jonathan.

"Darling," she would coo, "could you take me for a drive?" Jonathan was surprised, actually shocked at how well she had handled the tattoo and more importantly, the secrecy of it all.

"My car is in the shop," he shrugged.

"Well, use mine," she suggested.

"You have a car?" *Probably an old clunker*, he thought to himself.

"Yes, Jonathan, I am not without some means. It's in a storage garage a few miles south at Surfside. Let me see where that paper is."

She shuffled to her dresser and took out a shoebox full of old envelopes. She rooted around in it until she came up with a set of keys, an envelope with a numeric code and a return address, which she handed him with a smirk. "Here you go. I don't know what kind it is, but it is cream colored and it rides very well. You go ahead and use it until your car is ready." Naomi cut her eyes at him so that he wondered if she knew he was lying about having a car. "And then, tomorrow, let's go for a ride."

Chapter 17

He nodded stupidly. Miss Naomi Waterman had boggled his mind more than once since Christmas Eve. When he'd insisted that she allow him to have power of attorney, she had been more than willing and seemed grateful for the help. He'd been practically rubbing his hands together in anticipation of getting his hands on her considerable money. Then she dropped the bomb. "If you hold my power of attorney, then I want to hold yours. I can get my attorney to draw up the contracts and bring them out for us both to sign."

The last thing Timmy Lee wanted was a face-to-face meeting with an attorney. *What is Naomi doing with her own attorney?* Another shocker was that she had to see his tattoo every now and then, like every few days, and she wanted to touch it. *I have to redo the henna to keep it looking real. Naomi is starting to get on my nerves.*

Today, she'd pleaded, "Do come in the morning and let's go for a ride." He had said that he'd try, but he had a sermon to write. She'd dismissed him. After he left, she tottered out to the card game. "Yes, deal me in, Margaret. Jonathan is going to be busy this afternoon running some errands."

* * * * *

The girls were less curious than they had been. Naomi noticed. And they didn't tease her as much, at least about her having a boyfriend, and she was glad. *What they don't know won't hurt them,* she thought. She drifted away between turns. *I just love being in love, but it is the chase more than anything else. The thrill of it all is the chase.*

"Naomi, your turn." Margaret's voice came through the fog.

"Yes, yes." She fumbled her cards then played three aces, a four and five on Margaret's run of six-seven-eight, a king on Rosemary's three kings and turned her last card over on the discard pile. "Rummy." She grinned big enough that her missing upper side tooth space showed.

Margaret shook her head, "Still waters must run deep. Good job, Naomi."

* * * * *

Jonathan got an Uber to take him south on US-17 Business to Full Service Storage where he found Naomi's unit, an enclosed, climate-controlled garage. The keypad code handwritten on the envelope opened the unit's roll-up door. There was only one thing in the unit and as the door opened, Jonathan whistled between his teeth. A 2018 Cadillac CTS-V Sedan, cream-colored as promised, sparkled in the cool air. *What in the holy hell is Naomi doing with this race car?* He walked around the vehicle once, trailing his fingertips along the lines of the beautiful, sensuous car. Then, hungry to drive it, he slipped onto the leather upholstery, noted the 8-speed transmission and eased it out onto the highway. He had never driven anything as magnificent, even in the good years.

"Now, wasn't this worth the wait?" He praised himself aloud. "You were right to be patient and wait for the big one to bite. And this is just the beginning. You know she has money. She's probably got real estate, too." He turned on the Bose radio and enjoyed the surround sound, even sang along. "Finally, ole boy, you have hit the mother lode." He adjusted the power seat and turned on the cooling air ventilation so that a gentle breeze blew cool air up his back. After he cruised Ocean Boulevard from one end of Myrtle Beach to the other, he parked about a block from the chapel and walked home. Stretched out on his Army cot, he became more practical. He'd spent his last dollar on the Uber ride to Surfside. He was going to need gas money and food money and some new clothes, fine enough to be seen driving the Caddy. *A thousand bucks would be a good start. Hell, I'll do whatever the old bat wants for a thousand bucks and to keep the car. Massage her skinny back, French kiss her, please her however she wants pleased.* A shiver of repulsion helped him realize that he may or may not be able to meet her needs. But still, he vowed to try.

He dreamed about his mother that night. He relived her death, the look on her face as he strangled her. And he had done that just to shut her up. If he could be Naomi's beneficiary and had something to gain, he could help her into the next world happily. He snuggled under the warm covers. His anger was forgotten; he couldn't wait to take Naomi on a drive the next day.

* * * * *

Naomi chuckled as she dressed for bed. He was just child enough to enjoy that stupid car. As long as he did what she wanted, he could keep it. She imagined him holding the car door for her like Cinderella getting into her beautiful carriage. Then, he'd kiss her. She stretched her bony legs apart and flexed her hips against the silk of her gown, pretending that she was kissing his finger where the joint was missing. *So exciting to be part of the chase again*, she thought.

Chapter 18

Here's the Deal

Naomi was dressed fit to kill by the time Jonathan arrived to pick her up. She'd also made a phone call and expected a courier to drop off a cashier's check from Coastal Carolina, her downtown bank. She had planned a nice surprise for Jonathan. *That is, if he agreed to his part of the bargain.*

Margaret and her friends were in the breakfast room when Naomi glided by in a cloud of bath powder and perfume. Her tailored lavender pants suit fit perfectly and she had a sweater over one arm. She carried a fancy mini bag and big-rimmed square sunglasses were perched on her head, ready for a trip outside and the glare of the merciless South Carolina sun.

The women's heads turned in unison as she found a seat by the window. "Whoa, Baby." Margaret was the first to find her voice. "Naomi Waterman, I presume." She scooted her chair back from the table, grabbed her plate of eggs and toast, destined to grow cold, and moved to Naomi's table. "May I join you?"

Naomi looked up and nodded. "Do you think I look all right?"

Margaret rolled her eyes. "All right? Honey, really? You are a sugarplum, a tasty morsel with perfect packaging. Would you style me, Naomi? You are as put together a woman as I have ever seen."

"Well, I've had a few years to practice," she whispered, buttering her toast. "Not that I'd admit to more than 70." Both women laughed.

Naomi couldn't hear the buzz at other tables, but Margaret could. She made a mental note to tell those women to back off and let Naomi do whatever she was going to do. "Are you going out this morning? I hope so, it would be a pity to waste that outfit on us."

Naomi chewed a tiny bit of toast. She patted her mouth with the cloth napkin before she spoke, "Yes, I believe that Reverend Wesley is stopping by this morning for a drive."

Margaret felt an unexpected surge of pride in the tiny, lonely woman. "Now, Honey, you be careful with the Reverend. He may be a preacher, but he is still a man." Margaret waited for a response. Naomi took another tiny bite. "I'm just saying that you be careful and don't get into a situation that you can't control, if you know what I mean."

"Uh huh," Naomi answered while thinking, *I know exactly what you mean and I am counting on it.*

"And you let me know when you are leaving here with him and when you are coming back. You know Nurse Danvers doesn't keep a good sign-out book. People come and go around here whenever the mood hits them."

Naomi nodded again. *Counting on that, too,* she thought.

Margaret noticed Jonathan through the window, striding from the parking lot to the front entrance. "And behave yourself." Margaret squeezed Naomi's forearm, but she really wanted to grab her and take her back to her room away from what was surely going to end badly. Naomi moved her plate away and pushed in her chair before Jonathan entered the room.

Jonathan Wesley stopped in the breakfast room's arched doorway, took off his sunglasses and wiped them on a clean handkerchief. He was stalling as he waited to get his inside vision. Naomi could tell he was excited and assumed he was completely dazzled by the Cadillac. When his eyes rested on her, it was as if she dazzled him, too. A less honest woman would have pretended, for a second at least, that he was in love with her, but Naomi was cruelly honest with herself. He was clearly greedy and wanted more and more and always more. The car would pacify him for a few weeks, she figured, maybe months. After that he would want something else. In the back of her mind she could hear the scratching of her daddy's round top radio and Lefty Frizzell singing "If you got the money, Honey, I got the time," as Jonathan swaggered across the room to her. Funny the things one's mind held onto from childhood. She offered him her bent hand, and just as in her fantasies, he took it and pressed his lips to it. She hoped that she rose gracefully while the other residents watched.

"Your car awaits, Madame." He offered his arm and she took it and walked with him out of the room. Her friends applauded, as caught up in the magic of an old lady's dream as she was.

They spent the day traveling to the top beach attractions visible from the car. It was still early spring and although the sun was bright, the air had a cold bite to it.

"Is there any place you'd like to go first?" Jonathan inquired.

"You choose for me, Dear. I'm happy to just be with you."

So he took her to his Freedom Chapel and pointed out the improvements that he'd like to make if the church income ever permitted it. "The steeple could be modernized. I built it myself so there's no shortage of adoration for the Good Lord, but a store bought one would be nicer. And," he admitted, "the building could use a coat of paint." Naomi agreed. "And if you could see inside, I think you would agree that pews would add to the ambiance. Folding chairs are either cold or hot and rattle and screech on the concrete floor. Wooden pews would be more comfortable."

Naomi asked, "How many in your congregation?" Jonathan didn't dare tell her he hadn't preached a sermon in a month. He'd used sermon writing as an excuse to get away from her.

"Well, the numbers fluctuate. Between two and three dozen people would be a good guess."

"Do you have a governing body that pays your salary and the utilities?"

I wish, he thought, but answered, "Yes, Ma'am, but it is a very tight budget."

Then they drove to the famous Myrtle Beach Pavilion and parked where they could watch the people on the boardwalk as well as the waves pounding the beach. Naomi laid one hand in his and he patted it for what seemed like hours before his stomach growled.

"Jonathan, let's go to the Sonic for lunch." She seemed as excited as a little girl. Lunch was served: a chicken sandwich and a caramel shake for Naomi and a double cheeseburger, tater tots, and limeade for Jonathan. Then he drove south along the coast to Murrells Inlet where they parked near the Marshwalk and people watched.

Naomi dozed off in the luxury of the sun-filled Cadillac as Jonathan made up funny stories about the few people that were in sight. He quit talking when she started breathing deeply and whistling a little as she slept. There were blue and

Chapter 18

white herons in the shallow water and he watched them catch fish and gobble them up, silently cheering them on to eat more and more.

She spoke before she opened her eyes, which startled him, "Jonathan, my love?"

He flinched at the sound but played the role. "What is it, Naomi, what do you need?"

"I need to get back to Sea View. But, I have a deal to offer you." She opened her eyes and pushed herself up in the seat. "Has this day been pleasant for you?"

"Oh, yes. Very much so. Although, anywhere with you would be pleasant," he added as an afterthought. Naomi frowned, but went on.

"I would like to spend three days a week in a manner similar to today's outing." He started to speak and she interrupted. "Now, I know that you have your own professional obligations both at the nursing home and at the Freedom Chapel, so I would be willing to help you recover your lost time."

He perked up but could not decide whether to speak or not.

She went on, "I'm suggesting a stipend of $150 per day that you spend with me. You could use that for gasoline or living expenses or really, whatever." She gazed out the window. "And as our relationship develops, I insist on exclusiveness and shared legal authority and rights of survivorship."

Jonathan was stunned. "Does that mean I am your beneficiary and you are mine?"

"Yes. Whichever of us passes first would leave their worldly estate to the other."

"How would we consummate these arrangements?" Jonathan was nearly breathless. His heart was racing. He could hardly believe this was falling into his lap.

"Legal contract. I'll have my Myrtle Beach attorney draw it up and we could sign it privately and get it notarized."

Jonathan shook his head. "I don't want to think about a world without you." He was able to make his voice quiver.

"Sweet man." Naomi whispered and leaned towards him, lips pursed and heading towards his. Jonathan knew what was expected and he was no coward. Not for this kind of money. He sealed the deal with a puckered, dry kiss. Naomi fell back into her seat with her hand over the branded heart on her chest.

"Please take me home, Dear."

He didn't know whether to hurry and get rid of her or make his way back slowly, pretending to care. Finally, after some of both behaviors, he parked at the main entrance and hurried around to hold her door. She had him arrange the sweater around her shoulders, "The air-conditioning is such a shock coming in from the heat," she explained. "I can find my own way," she said, "but do stop by in the morning and I'll have a check prepared, you dear, dear man." She cradled his face in her twisted hand.

Another car had pulled up behind him and he had no choice but to clear the drive. He apologized and drove slowly away. She thought she heard the car radio suddenly blast loudly. She understood and wasn't amused.

The words of Lefty Frizzell's hit haunted her as she walked down the tile hallway to her room, "But if you run short of money, I'll run short of time. 'Cause you with no more money, honey, I've got no more time." *Daddy was mean to sing that to poor mother all those years ago.*

Chapter 19

Federal Court

Jonas and Stella drove up to Charleston, West Virginia, the state capitol, for a Federal District Court hearing. Mountain Top Pipeline had requested permission to begin pipeline construction by March 1 even though all landowners had not yet agreed to easements. They cited irreparable financial damages if trees were not cut down and digging the trench did not begin as soon as possible.

Jonas and Stella were early that icy morning, but the security screeners were even earlier and wasted no time in idle chatter. There was no Good morning, no chitchat. Strictly business. Both Akpiks caused the metal detector to ding. They removed their belts and walked through again without a word. When they made it upstairs to the courtroom through

marble hallways with sky lit rotundas, they had their pick of seats on the wooden pews in the spectator section. The room was impressive: high ceilings, ornate woodwork, big spaces between the front podium where the judge would sit and the lawyers' tables plus another big space between the lawyers and the spectators.

"It's big as a gym." Jonas spoke with reverence.

"Or a church." Stella countered.

"Depends on where you worship, I guess." Stella twisted her face at him and he backed off and tried to smooth things over. "But, dang, an awesome room no matter where you come from."

"Feels like sacred ground." Stella closed her eyes and clung to the back of the front pew to let it all soak in.

They chose seats midway back in the spectator section and settled in time to watch the other spectators enter. Men in bib overalls and women with knit caps pulled over their ears came in. Stella knew several of them, had interacted on email and in activist groups, but hadn't actually met them live and in person. The seven attorneys and their entourages also entered, all wearing dark suits.

The bailiff asked everyone to stand as the judge entered. Judge Jack Cunningham was ninety-two years old and his entrance was slow. He seemed to think about each step.

The only witness all morning was Budwick Thornhill, the project manager for Mountain Top Pipeline's current project. MTP's female attorney was questioning him. The questions and answers were well choreographed; they flowed smoothly.

Jonas nudged Stella during the proceedings. "He's asleep," he mouthed and nodded towards the judge.

Stella mouthed back, "No, he is not." Sure enough, the MTP suit made a misstep and Judge Cunningham spoke up.

"The question is how many jobs will the pipeline provide and you answered 6,000. Now, I want to know how many permanent jobs will be added to the area in question."

"Do you mean after construction is complete, Your Honor? That would be about 40 jobs, Sir."

"And of those 40 jobs, how many would be located in the southern district of West Virginia; the four counties of Nicholas, Greenbrier, Summers, and Monroe, the southern district, which is the only area over which this court has jurisdiction." The judge's voice had gotten louder.

"About 20, Your Honor, 20."

"That number came a long way down from 6,000 to 20." Jonas whispered, chuckling.

Judge Cunningham leaned back and appeared to snooze again. The attorney asked Mr. Thornhill how MTP would be irreparably harmed if they were not allowed to begin construction immediately.

"We'd lose $40-$50 million every month we are delayed."

A gasp from the spectators proved they were paying attention and seemed to alert the judge, who spoke up and reviewed the fact that MTP's plan submitted to the Federal Energy Regulatory Commission showed construction starting in August, not March, and that the contracts to transport natural gas did not begin until the following year. "So, you would not be **losing** $40-$50 million a month, you would simply be delayed in collecting it until your already anticipated and advertised starting date. Is that correct, Mr. Thornhill?"

"Yes, Sir, but we could be earning that money sooner."

"Do you understand the meaning of the word irreparable, Mr. Thornhill?" Judge Cunningham was shouting, then he took a breath and spoke quietly as if he were only talking to the witness, but everyone in the room heard him. "It is in the wording of your request, for God's sake."

As if the outburst had exhausted him, the judge dismissed the witness and called for a lunch break. Stella and Jonas stepped out of the courthouse into sleet that made pecking noises against umbrellas and windbreakers. Stella held the lapels of her fleece-lined denim jacket together as they jaywalked across three lanes of traffic. They noticed a group of men in suits and overcoats crossing at the same time. "Don't look now, Jonas, but those are some of the lawyers representing land owners."

"Mr. Sweeney?" Stella hurried to the sidewalk to catch up with the group.

"Yes, Ma'am." One man stopped, turned and the group paused their conversation.

"That pipeline is going across our sheep field and we don't want it to. Please keep giving 'em hell."

Mr. Sweeney took off his hat despite the sleet. "Ma'am, that's all they deserve." His group laughed and they continued walking up the street to a restaurant.

"Can't believe you spoke up to that man. He probably took you for a shy little kitten from the farm," Jonas said with a grin.

Stella bristled until she saw him grinning. "Oh, you." She swatted at Jonas's shoulder.

Chapter 19

"Somebody probably should tell him you are so mean that you go bear hunting with a switch." She swatted at him again. Jonas grabbed her hand and they ran together inside the first café they came to. They found a table, ordered sandwiches, and chatted about the lone witness and the dozen or so lawyers that represented so many landowners, and the unimaginable amount of money that MTP stood to make.

After lunch, the court session drug on until after dark. Mr. Sweeney got to cross-examine the project manager and threw several monkey wrenches in his testimony. After that, each attorney had chosen one landowner to testify as to the "irreparable damage" they were suffering with the loss of their land. Most of them were farmers and all were plainspoken.

"If I can't raise and sell livestock and grain, I can't support my family."

"My boy will be our family's fifth generation on this land."

"Blasting will change the groundwater and will probably affect the wells and springs that people and animals must have."

"My husband, God rest his soul, and I worked a lifetime to pay off our farm. How can it be taken from us?"

"What will be our children's inheritance? They can't live on top of a pipeline."

When the court session ended, the judge didn't rule. He explained that he would decide in the next few days after he had time to study the facts of the case. Spectators applauded and the general feeling in the back pews of the courtroom was festive. People laughed and visited as they put on their coats, sure he would never allow such a thing.

On the two-hour-long trip home on the dangerous, poorly engineered West Virginia turnpike, Stella and Jonas revisited every testimony. "It looks good, Stella, it really does. I can't imagine the judge allowing the greedy fools to have access to land on which they haven't even gotten permission for easements."

"Yeah, that judge was on mistakes like white on rice. I don't think MTP scored any points at all with him. $50 million a month! Shame on them for the little bit of money they are paying for land."

They got a good night's sleep that night, and for the next week, until the judge rendered his decision: allowing MTP to begin tree-cutting and pipeline construction on properties being taken under eminent domain, without the owner's permission.

Chapter 20

Decision from the Judge

Stella and Jonas got a copy of Judge Cunningham's decision in the mail the day after it was issued:

> MEMORANDUM OPINION AND ORDER granting Mountain Top's motions to strike; denying as stricken the landowners' motions to dismiss; denying the landowners' MOTION for stay of proceedings; granting Mountain Top's MOTION for Partial Summary Judgment and immediate access to and possession of the easements condemned in Nicholas, Greenbrier, Summers, and Monroe Counties, West Virginia; the court directs Mountain Top to post the deposit and security as directed, which is a predicate to Mountain Top's right to possess the condemned property and begin construction by the cutting of trees by whatever means necessary and as further directed and set forth more fully herein.
> Signed by Judge Jackson Cunningham.

"There are no words to sum up how much I despise that judge." Stella took deep breaths to stave off the nausea. She was physically ill. Her joints ached and her head had pounded all night. Elbows on the table, she sat with her face over a steaming cup of cocoa, trying to still her stomach by savoring the rich chocolate fumes.

"I believe you've got the Pipeline Flu, Babe." Jonas pulled

up the chair across from her. "You want some eggs and ham? I'm cooking."

"Sure, I need to fuel up. Plus I need some information."

"Like what?"

She thought before she spoke. "I'll tell you one thing for sure: those are our trees and I am not going to welcome the pipeline workers with chain saws to cut them down. Jonas, they are white oaks and they have to be over two hundred years old. I looked up how to tell. You multiply the diameter in inches by five to get the age in years.

"Those trees saw people riding in carriages drawn by horses on these same mountain roads, they watched the railroads being built and heard men singing as they pounded in the spikes. Andrew Jackson was president when they were saplings, Jonas. They saw slaves run north in the night and watched boys in Confederate uniforms march by. They were here before this land was even West Virginia."

"I don't know, Babe. There is a court order to cut them down. How do we stop that?"

She sipped the cocoa. "I need to know what I can do to save the trees that has the shortest jail time served as a penalty. My second priority is not getting hurt."

Jonas hadn't realized the depth of her intentions. He forgot about scrambling eggs for the time being.

Stella went on, "I think it would be a bad idea to be armed, at least so that the gun could be seen. Would probably cause more trouble."

"I agree 100%. You and that Pink Lady of yours scare me."

"I am not non-violent, Jonas, not in my heart. Sometimes, I think that shooting something might be the shortest distance to a solution for a lot of problems. But, I don't want to spend more than a night or two in jail. And I worry if I would have to use the bathroom in front of somebody. I can't even do that in the Wal-Mart bathroom when I hear noises in other stalls." She looked away. "I have to wait until everybody leaves. My bladder just won't empty if somebody else is listening. Can't go." She sighed.

Jonas did not point out that there could be bigger problems in jail than this. He did not remind her that there would most likely be a fine or that convicted felons could not have a gun. He decided to heat up some ham and eggs.

The phone rang. It was Tisha. "Hey, woman, heard about your dumb ass judge. He is either stupid or corrupt. Now that it is done, what are we going to do about it?"

"I don't know. I just know that I have to do something. I don't know what. Those trees belong to us not to Budwick Thornhill!" Stella was floundering in her anger.

"The guy's name is Budwick? Is he a Yankee or something? Just saying, he sounds like he's not from around here. I don't reckon it matters. What matters is what are we going to do about it?"

Stella chewed her fingernail. "I was thinking about having a sit-in or maybe it would be a sit-out because it will be outside. Just sitting in front of the trees so they couldn't cut them down. What do you think?"

"Chained or unchained?"

"Unchained. Definitely unchained."

"You know that they will call the police?"

"I've taught all those deputies in Sunday school and Sheriff Elmer wouldn't dare use a cattle prod on me, do you think?"

"Shoot, Stella, your Jonas would be crazier than a sprayed roach if anybody hit you up with a cattle prod." Even though she knew Jonas couldn't hear the other side of the conversation, Stella looked at him before she dared to laugh.

"Gosh, Tish, what I am most worried about is that I can't pee in jail with someone else listening."

"Good God, woman, that's what you are worried about? Is that why you never go to the bathroom at the same time as we do? Whoo-whee, learn something new every day."

"Okay, Tish, you willing?"

"Yep. We got ourselves an E-vent!"

The conversation continued and they talked about who else would come and how they would know when the lumberjacks would be there and if they would be single and Eliza came, maybe she would go for one of them. Tisha would post it on Facebook and Stella would get the tree cutting schedule from MTP and unbeknownst to him, Jonas was volunteered to put a couple of deer stands in trees so they could actually sit in the trees. They'd get Tisha's Aunt Willie to cater picnic food for those in the trees and Eliza would probably go get them in Union when they made bail. Oh, yeah, would Joey pay Tisha's bail? They decided that anyone who participated needed to arrange their own bail and ride home from jail.

Chapter 20

"So shall it be." Stella was back on track. "Thanks, Tisha. I feel better about trying, might not amount to anything, but we gotta try."

Tisha said, "Love you."

"Love you, too," then she turned to Jonas who had cooked and eaten a plate of ham and eggs during the call. He pointed his fork at the empty plate and questioned her with his look.

"Oh, yes, I'd love some, Jonas. Oh, Jonas, it's going down."

He turned to the stove so she didn't see him grinning. If one woman could stop a 300-mile-long pipeline, his money was on Stella. Just as she had predicted with the airplane crash story, this was about to get real.

Chapter 21

Springtime in the South

Jonathan Wesley and Naomi were welcoming springtime in South Carolina. Their car trips were ranging a bit farther as days went on. First, they extended the miles down to Surfside Beach, where they walked up the ramp to the pier and had French toast and mimosas at the Surf Café. A week later and another few miles, they were at Garden City Beach. Jonathan walked her into the arcade where she begged to play Skee-Ball. She earned 100 tickets from her five-dollar investment and chose a pocketful of candy as her prize. Then, they ventured a little farther, to Murrells Inlet again, where they found lively seafood restaurants. She slept all the way home that evening.

Chapter 21

They'd watched the trees bud out, and by mid-March, saw the blooms of flowering shrubs and trees. Naomi clapped her hands at lacy purple blooms and called them "fairy-like." She squealed with delight at delicate flowers that looked like white tiny popcorn balls and wished aloud that she could smell them. Jonathan jumped a hedge, broke a delicate stem, and ran back to the car for Naomi to enjoy the fragrance.

They visited Brookgreen Gardens and saw massive sculptures. Jonathan tried to decide how they could be stolen and decided it would be too much work to load and haul and find a buyer. He took her to Huntington State Park at dusk and shined a big flashlight on and around the water there to show Naomi the shining eyes of scores of 'gators. She was speechless and he realized that it was a bad idea to show her if pushing her into the marsh was an option. *Oh, well,* he thought, *there are plenty of other ways for her to go.*

Pink and purple azaleas lined garden borders. Jonathan drove through upscale housing developments for Naomi to watch the spring growth of landscaped flower blooms. In the meantime, the grass grew brighter and greener as the temperatures grew warmer.

"I don't remember the grass being that green when I was a kid." Jonathan revisited his childhood from time to time as Naomi revisited hers. He shared some truths but created affluence and status in his childhood home, a dairy farm near Atlanta where there was none.

"You probably had other things to do besides notice the grass." Naomi tried to learn more about "her" man. "Did you have any brothers or sisters?"

The sun was warm and the sky was blue and Jonathan was in a good mood, so he told a rare truth. "Yes, I had a little sister, she goes by Stella now. Haven't seen her for a while. We were never close." He grimaced as he thought of Stella trying to shoot him, twice in recent years. He hadn't forgotten her mother-in-law beating him with an iron skillet, either.

"Honey, I'm sorry to ask about painful things." Naomi tried to soften what she correctly believed to be his memory of a terrible relationship. "I have an older brother. He was crippled." Her voice grew curt and cold. "He got all the attention from my parents and had his own live-in teacher while I had to go away to school. You know, he was a boy and thus important and all that."

Jonathan was so stunned that he turned to stare at Naomi and nearly hit an approaching truck head-on. *Someone to share her fortune with?* After the swerve and Naomi's scream, he pulled over to get control of himself. He breathed deeply several times and turned back to her. He could see that she was trembling with fear. "I'm okay," she assured him, "but let's go on back right away." Jonathan realized that this could be a good ploy to end a visit and filed it away for future use.

Naomi couldn't figure out why he had turned to her with such anger, and also filed it away for more thought.

Jonathan escorted Naomi to her room that afternoon after he'd found a parking place near the door. "Let's go to Charleston on Friday," she whispered as she clung to his arm. He led her down the hallway to her room past the wheelchairs and sofas where residents sat. He nodded to them. She loved her friends greeting her; it pleased her to finally be the center of attention.

At her insistence, he'd dropped his musical presentation on the days he took her out. "So we are not on any ol' schedule," she told him. He'd done it, but he longed to be on a schedule that got him done early enough to cruise the boulevard in the early evening. She had lengthened several outings and now it looked like they were going ninety miles south to Charleston, South Carolina. He didn't know where she thought this was going to end, but he expected a tragic accident to happen in the near future. He just needed to take care of the paperwork, the survival and power of attorney documents. He'd ask her on the way to Charleston. Lord knows there would be time on that day, more time with her than he wanted. He was getting sick of car rides with her.

In fact, he was dog-tired of Naomi and his church. He was getting weary of the whole preaching thing and fed up with doing the repairs and upgrades that Naomi had financed. On one of his days off from Naomi, he was putting the last coat of paint on the exterior when Patsy, his self-appointed ministry sponsor, stopped by.

"Hey there Jonathan, the building is looking good. How's the spirit on the inside?" He climbed down the ladder, looking tanned beneath the spatters of white paint.

"You are a sight for sore eyes, Sister Patsy." He ran his hand through his designer haircut and winked, all the time thinking, *more like my eyes get sore looking at you, you big oaf of a woman.*

Patsy clasped her hands together in delight, which got her sagging underarms swinging. Her smile pulled her lips back exposing her upper and lower gums. *I have seen better looking cows,* Jonathan told himself. But he knew who had buttered his bread and he wasn't quite ready to move on, so he played the role. "Our congregation offered enough to make the new steeple and this paint job possible, so I guess the spirit inside is just soaring, Sister Patsy." He winked again.

Patsy beamed. "I am so proud of you and your ministry, Jonathan." She moved her handbag from one hand to the other and shifted her weight. "But we need to talk."

He stuffed his brush into a plastic bag, replaced the lid on the paint bucket and swept his arm towards the door, "After you, my dear."

She walked in front of him, hand on mouth, then entered and gushed about how good the interior of the chapel looked, "Oh, my, this is nice and fresh." There were ten cushioned pews now and a white paneled altar up front. She sat down on a pew. "Jonathan, we have a problem."

"Well, we'll give it to the Lord, Sister Patsy."

"I think the Lord has given it back, Jonathan." She sat up straight. "One of the conditions of using this building is covering liability, fire, wind, and flood insurance. I promised the owner that a policy would be in place and I have been paying it, but winter collections were down, even more than most winters, and my church can't pay it anymore."

"Should we pray, Patsy?"

"Yes, please."

They bowed their heads. Jonathan took her hands and began, "Our Heavenly Father, we are grateful for your many gifts and for your love. Have mercy on us all, for we have sinned." He opened one eye to see how Patsy took that. She was nodding. *Cool,* he thought. "We come to you today to lay our financial burden at your feet. We ask for the money to pay the insurance policy on this, your building. Lord, we have faith, we believe in your goodness and mercy. Lead us to a solution to this challenge, Lord, and help us know your will. In the name of Jesus, your precious son, we ask. Amen."

"Amen," Patsy added and squeezed Jonathan's hands. "Monthly installments are due on the fifteenth of every month. $247 a month. Thank you."

Jonathan looked her in the eyes and shamelessly lied, "I will be in touch when I get the money. Don't worry about a thing, Patsy. God will provide." He decided not to tell her that he had a cellphone and give her his number, it might be an entanglement later. Instead, on impulse, he kissed her on the forehead.

She blushed and touched her forehead where his lips touched her.

"You are such a good man, Jonathan. A man of God."

After she left, he laughed bitterly, realizing, *time is ticking and I need to act sooner than I had planned. Leave the church. Get Naomi's legal crap in order, and do away with her.* He had been holding his breath. God would provide. He breathed again.

Chapter 22

Hope of Love

Nurse Danvers hadn't grumbled at the noisy card games lately. The formidable nurse seemed to ignore their loud laughter and voices these days, when just a few weeks ago she would have investigated and enforced a quieter sunroom. Margaret stopped by the nurse's counter after lunch to find out what was going on. "Oh, Nurse Danvers, good afternoon."

The nurse looked up. "Thank you kindly and hello to you," she said and hung up the file folder she'd been updating. "I've been meaning to talk to you about something, Miss Margaret. Do you have a minute?"

"Yes, Ma'am. What's on your mind?"

Nurse Danvers came around the counter and whispered, "Let's go find a quiet office." Margaret followed, looking left and right, a little like a schoolgirl in trouble going to the principal's office.

The nurse pushed the door of an administrative office open. "The dietician is not here today, we can talk without interruption in her office." She sat in a wingback chair and patted the matching one next to her. Margaret sat down.

There was an extended quiet. Margaret, puzzled, just watched Nurse Danvers wriggle to get comfortable in the chair and struggle with her choice of words before blurting out, "I'm worried sick about Naomi Waterman." Her eyes met Margaret's and no one blinked.

"Why?" Margaret figured it was her continuing relationship with Reverend Wesley, but she wanted to get the facts straight.

"She is slipping in and out of this facility at will," she crossed her arms, "and at all hours. We have couriers and lawyers visiting every other day. She is conducting business of some sort from her room."

"What kind of business?"

Nurse Danvers shrugged. "I don't know. It concerns me."

Margaret took some time to choose her words carefully. "Do you think she's selling drugs? A prostitution operation? Come on, now." Then, she spoke more kindly, "Danvers, she seems to be in love and is truly having a good time. Have you noticed how nice she looks these days? And how happy she is?"

"It does not seem appropriate for a woman her age to be keeping company with such a man. And him a preacher. We, here at Sea View are responsible for her wellbeing. You know, she is staying out to the wee hours at least once a week and then sleeps through breakfast. That can't be healthy, it could take years off her life."

"Oh, but what about her quality of life?" Margaret's eyes twinkled as she leaned forward. "And she is inspirational, she's given a dozen old ladies hope." The nurse's eyes widened. Margaret went on, "Hope of life. Hope of love. Memories of their own loves. She's given them a reason to get out of bed and change out of their nightgowns and squirt a little perfume behind each ear. Some of the ladies even think that they could woo Reverend Wesley away from her, although they give it more thought than effort."

Nurse Danvers wrung her hands, "But she is in my care. What if something happens to her? A car wreck? Or a, a, a heart attack? "

Margaret was worried too, but for a different reason. "Have you notified her family?"

Danvers pounded both fleshy fists on the arm of her chair. "There is nobody to call. She listed 'Penny' as an employee, but I've never met her or him."

Margaret remembered hearing Naomi mention Penny. "Employee? Do we have an address for this Penny person?"

"I can look it up. He's somewhere up north, maybe West Virginia."

Margaret was deep in thought. "I'd like to get that address and phone number, that is, if you are allowed to share it. What can I do to help?"

Eagerly, Danvers leaned forward, "Keep an eye and ear out for her. If she gets herself in trouble, let me know and we can rescue her. I would feel so much better if there were two of us watching out."

"I think it is safe to say that there are ten or more of us paying attention to her every move. I don't think Naomi is in any danger except for the inevitability of her heart getting broken by a younger man and maybe losing some pin money." As she did at the card table, Margaret kept her information cards close to her chest.

"But you'll tell me if she needs help?"

Margaret laughed out loud. "Oh, I sure will, but I think she can handle this situation better than you or I could. Let's let her have a little fun."

The nurse sighed with satisfaction. "You are not like our other residents, Margaret. You have something else, a presence. Can't put my finger on it, but I trust you, at least on this one. What did you do, before here, I mean?"

"This and that. Office manager for a lawyer, house mother at a school for girls, hostess at a restaurant." Margaret was flat out lying now, just seeing how much the nurse would believe.

The nurse nodded, seeming to buy it all. "I do appreciate being able to share this with you. Obviously, it is confidential." She hurried out of the office.

"Obviously," Margaret muttered and remained seated for another minute before strolling back to the girls in the sunroom. She felt for the deck of cards in her pocket, and feeling the familiar box, brightened at the prospect of a lively card game to start the afternoon.

They had gathered at the regular table and Naomi was holding court, showing them a big blue gemstone ring that Jonathan had given her. If the truth was known, she'd only asked Jonathan to put it on her finger. She had owned it for fifty years, but she liked her friends to think that he'd given it to her. It also helped with her dignity as she had invested several thousand dollars in his church and his stipend during the last few weeks. *Happiness is priceless,* she told herself often and had pretty much convinced herself.

The gang was raring to go. Rummy was a priority of the day, equaled only by the girls' continuing interest in Naomi's love life.

Chapter 23

Pipeline and Trees

Stella had become so stressed and worried over the pipeline that Jonas was becoming stressed and worried about her. He quizzed Ben around the coffee pot at work, "How can I get her to back off? Man, she is deep into this fight. She went down to Doc's Sporting Goods in Christiansburg and bought two tree stands, nice ones for deer hunting, and got me to put them up in two of our biggest oak trees. All those trees are in the way of the pipeline. When we get the notice that MTP is coming to cut them down, she and some of her friends are going to sit in the deer stands to protect the trees."

"Let me guess, she has talked Tisha and Eliza into it, too?"

"Yep, yep. Sella has even called the sheriff to tell him exactly where the trees are when the time comes to arrest her."

Chapter 23

"Poor Elmer, I want to watch him and his men arrest Stella and get her out of a tree."

"Ben, you don't know the half of it. They have food delivery and phone charging all planned out for the tree-sitters. They have cameras and megaphones and signs and the phone numbers to call newspapers and TV stations when the time comes." Jonas looked at the clock and saw that he had spent too much time in the coffee room already, but he needed to vent a bit more. "Have you ever heard of a 'GirlFlo' device, Ben?"

"Nope." Ben stirred his coffee slowly, grinning with anticipation.

"They cost twenty bucks." Jonas shook his head. "I couldn't believe they existed. They are little pink gizmos that fit girls so they can pee without sitting down."

Ben laughed so hard that Jonas forgot the awkwardness of the whole situation. Between laughs, Ben choked out, "Probably a good thing to have if you are a girl and planning a long stay in a tree stand." Then, they both shook their heads again, mostly at modern technology which rocked their world pretty often.

"Whew, that Stella thinks of everything." Jonas nodded in agreement and sipped his coffee.

Then it occurred to Ben that Jonas was not part of the action. He knew better, being familiar with Stella's determination and organizational skills. "What's your job?"

"I am supposed to go get them when they get arrested. May need a cattle trailer to haul all these people," he grumbled. "Should we have one of those things where people that care about somebody sit down with them and explain why they need to quit doing whatever they are doing? They love them all right, but are trying to help them. What is that called?"

"An intervention?"

"Yeah, and they tell them to their face how unhealthy this thing is and how pointless?" Jonas knew as the words left his mouth that he was the one suggesting a pointless activity.

"Some people say that the person in question needs to hit bottom before an intervention stands a chance of working."

"Could happen if she uses that thing to pee from a deer stand." Both men chuckled again.

Ben sobered up first. "Have you ever gotten Stella to do anything she didn't want to do?" He knew Jonas's worry was forcing his laughter and honored his friend's concerns. The answer was obvious to them both.

Jonas shrugged in absolute defeat and moved on to another subject that was bothering him. "She's visited all the landowners on the pipeline corridor in Monroe County, at least all of them that she can find. Been up some hollers where I didn't even know there were houses. She's spent hours with these people. Like that old song says, she 'knows all of their children and all of their names.' When this pipeline comes through, she thinks people are going to join the fight, but I am not so sure. A few of them have taken the money, and the part of their land that is affected is a long way from the house or on a steep grade that they can't use for anything anyway. Clear to me that Stella cares the most."

"You can't fault her for trying, Jonas."

"Yeah, I know, it's just another way she is gonna get her heart broke." Jonas suddenly remembered a conversation from earlier in the week. "Hey, there are three people that she still can't find; they are out-of-state owners that have no addresses on record." He brightened, "You might know them. I'll get their names and see if they look familiar to you."

"Yeah, I can do that." Ben knew everybody on the mountain for miles around and from years ago. He slapped his buddy on the back, glad to be able to offer something in the way of help. They took their cooling cups of coffee to their respective desks.

Jonas felt better after admitting to Ben that he was worried. He had pretty much known from the start that the pipeline was coming no matter what the residents did. The system favored the deep pockets of the big spending corporations, that much he knew for sure.

That same day, the notice came in the mail. Workers from Mountain Top Pipeline hired to remove trees were coming the week of March 25. Stella shivered as she looked at the envelope, guessing what it held even before she ripped it open.

Then, she checked the weather for Monday, March 25. Sunny and warm. Good, the rain gear and tarps wouldn't be needed on the first day. They still had the weekend before taking to the trees. Her personal things were nearly ready; food, books, phones, extra camera, supplies, notebook and several pens and pencils for puzzles. She started making phone calls. *Tisha may not be able to get off work*, but Stella knew she would try. *Oh, Jonas.* She'd tell him when he came home from work, no point in worrying him just yet.

Stella completed her calls, then kicked up the footstool part of the recliner. She was half excited and half scared by the upcoming tree-sitting. It felt a lot like running away on graduation night. She hadn't known then how it would turn out, but she knew she had to do something. *Look how that worked out*, she told herself. *A new life. Jonas. Life on this beautiful mountain. Change can be good.* Then, for some reason, she thought about Timmy Lee. *He would be a good fit to work with Mountain Top Pipeline*, she thought. *They both are greedy, have no consideration for those around them, even for Mother Earth, and no eye for the future or the consequences of their actions. Yep, if he's alive out there somewhere, and surely he is, this is his kind of evil.*

She pushed the footstool back in place and sprang up. There was too much good in the world to sit and think about wickedness. A need for action replaced her nervousness and resolve replaced her fear.

Chapter 24

Tree-Sitting Eve

The weekend before the tree sitting was to begin was filled with sweetness. First, Jonas brought home fresh flowers from Food Lion.

"Oh, my word! Flowers! For me?" Stella gushed and threw her arms around her husband.

"Just a little preview, spring is coming. These low temperatures will be a memory in a few days. Remember, 'Come what may, May will come!'"

In answer, Stella practically danced around the room, gathering up snippers and a container, then trimming the ends of the stems and arranging them in her favorite crystal vase, humming the whole time.

"These look and smell so good. The bright colors just pop and I bet the whole house will smell like flowers in a few hours. I love them, Jonas." She started taking ingredients from the refrigerator. "Now, you sit down and talk to me while I cook. There will be your favorites tonight: meat loaf, green beans, and mashed potatoes."

"Oh, yeah? To what do I owe such special treatment?" He was grinning. Ben sure nailed it when he advised him to bring home flowers.

"Because you are you and I love you." She bustled around mixing eggs and ketchup with the ground beef and shaping the meat into a dome shaped loaf in the black iron skillet. "You've heard that the MTP people have scheduled our trees to be cut down starting on Monday?"

"No, I knew it was coming, but didn't realize it was now. Did they serve notice?"

Chapter 24

"Yep, in the mailbox this afternoon." She put the meatloaf in the oven and readied a pan full of frozen biscuits, then washed the potatoes to peel. She joined Jonas at the kitchen table with a cake pan of potatoes and a pot half full of water. She peeled as she spoke, "So, I am going up in one tree stand and Tisha is going up in the other. We have good sleeping bags and books and extra phone chargers. Eliza is delivering Aunt Willie's food every evening and Aunt Willie herself is bringing lunches. We have snacks for breakfast, cell phones, did I say that already? Would you be available by phone next week?"

"Azaa, woman, if you are going to be in a tree, I am going to be there, all right." The Native speech patterns and words of his childhood emerged when he was emotional. "You might katak from the tree, you might chill and get sick, you might ... " Jonas ran out of words.

"And I might stop a pipeline." She put the cut-up potatoes on to boil. "At least I will know that I tried. You remember that movie that you like so much, Shenandoah?"

"Yeah. I know, I know, when Jimmy Stewart says, 'If we don't do, we are not trying.'" He held his head in his hands.

Stella laughed, "Not exactly. Charlie Anderson, played by that precious Jimmy Stewart, says, 'If we don't try, we don't do. And if we don't do, why are we here on this Earth?' I aim to try, Jonas Akpik. They are not going to cut down those trees without me being there trying to stop them."

He rose from the table, unsure about whether to retreat out the back door or go on upstairs to be alone, when Stella jumped up to meet him.

"Jonas, look at me." She gave him time to look her up and down. "I am at peace now. This is what I want to do. I feel so much better now that it is happening than all these months waiting for it to begin. The airplane has finally crashed. This is real."

"What is real is that you are putting yourself in danger. Over a couple of trees. I waited too long for you, Stella, and I can't stand the thought that I could lose you. Over this, over trees. That damn pipeline could have the whole farm before I would want one hair on your head bothered."

Stella froze. "What? You are worried about our sheriff and deputies. Please. That's nothing to worry about. You know Elmer won't let his men hurt me." She finally moved to him and melted into his arms.

"I better turn off the potatoes." She whispered into his chest. "The beans will be okay in the crock pot and the meat loaf will cut off when it is done." Then they went upstairs.

Later that night, they came back downstairs for supper, laughing at each other, and making bad jokes about trees.

Stella reviewed what needed to be done on the farm in the coming week, which ewes hadn't delivered and what pills Buddy needed to take to help his inflamed knee, and what to do if the chicken coop door got stuck.

"Better make a list and spell it out pretty plain."

She looked at him in amazement. "If it isn't clear, just hike on up to the trees and ask, knothead."

"Leaf me alone." He grabbed her and rubbed her back.

"Enough of that. We need to rest up, we have two days of work to get ready for the tree-sitting."

"I wooden know." Jonas tried to keep a straight face but couldn't, and he chuckled as he followed his wife up the steps, back to bed.

They both fell asleep quickly, Jonas wrapped around Stella, the kind of sleep where you don't move until waking. She woke first, entangled in his arms. Carefully, she tried to move them to escape to the bathroom. He pretended to be asleep until he got tickled and started shaking with laughter. Stella slapped his bare chest good-naturedly and pushed him away. "I was trying to be nice and not wake you, but I have to have some re-leaf."

"I'm root-ing for you, Girl, and for your toile-trees." Stella laughed so hard she barely made it to the bathroom in time.

When she slid back under the covers, he got up. When he was nearly out of the room, Stella rolled over to face him, "May the forest be with you."

"Now, that's just dumb, Stella, tree-mendously dumb." He waved and disappeared down the hallway as she covered her face with a pillow trying to think of a comeback.

They worked hard on Saturday. After two trips to Boggess's Hardware Store, a series of pulleys and ropes was rigged to each tree stand, coolers were packed with non-perishables, gallons of water were transported along with bedding and straps to secure the tree-dweller while sleeping. They pitched a tent nearby to keep supplies dry and out of the wind and packed small items in dry bags in case of rain. Jonas used extra stakes to secure the bottom of the tent; he knew the power of the wind on the high points of the mountain.

Chapter 24

Stella wanted to go to church the next day, so Jonas went with her. She was bold enough to ask the congregation for prayers to help her to be strong enough to outlast the pipeline. There was weak applause. This was close to bringing politics into the church, never a good idea. She explained to Jonas that three years ago, most of the church people had believed Timmy Lee when he called her a thief, so she didn't lose much sleep over what they thought. She did want the prayers of the others, though; it couldn't hurt. Praying in church always seemed more effective to her than praying anywhere else which was the main reason she wanted to go to the services today.

Tisha and Joey came up on Sunday afternoon to check out the set-up and to drop off some things for the days to come. Joey kept on shaking his head as he looked around. He finally voiced his fear, "What about bears?"

Jonas looked at Stella, "Yeah, Babe, what's the plan for bears?" He kept on pulling ties tight on garbage bags full of extra clothing. In answer, Stella pulled the Pink Lady out of her sleeping bag and fired it overhead. The dogs yipped and ran.

Joey covered his ears, "Lord God, Stella, can't you just say you have a gun?"

"I been wanting to shoot it off, kinda like marking my territory. Sorry about the noise. I had forgotten how loud she is."

Tisha just laughed. "Any more questions, Hon?"

Joey shook his head no and remarked, "Reminds me of a story that my mom used to tell."

"Here we go, Stella." Tisha shook her finger at Joey, "Now we're in for a story."

Joey pulled up a cooler to sit on. "Well, it happened right here in Lindside years ago. There was a man whose wife traveled a lot for work. In those days, it might have been a trip to Beckley and she had to stay all night. In other words, she didn't travel far, but sometimes she was gone for a couple of nights. Her husband was a lot of fun but he didn't like to cook, so when she was gone, he'd dress up like a hobo in dirty raggedy clothes and wipe his face with dirt and go knock on doors and ask for food. Of course, everybody knew who he was, but they didn't let on and gave him a plate of food. He thought he was pretty clever to trick all his friends and neighbors and nobody ever told his wife on him."

"Is this some of your people?"

"Naah, you don't know him, Tish, and don't ask me a dozen more times because it isn't important." He continued, "That started being too easy and he was looking for a bigger and better prank to pull. It was the heat of summer and he heard that a bunch of women were going berry picking up near the Low Gap on Peters Mountain. Right over there," he pointed. "Now this was during the time when women wore light cotton house dresses in the summer, the kind with buttons up the front and a matching belt. Most of the old girls had made their clothes out of flowered flour sacks. They had a good time, talking and singing and filling their buckets with big blackberries. This particular blackberry patch was big, probably two acres of bushes with little paths through it. And it had been there for years, so there were older bushes, taller than a man's head and young, smaller bushes in the undergrowth. Well, this guy had heard the women talking about berry picking the day before, so he got up early and carried a big grizzly bear hide that he used as a rug."

"Where in the world would somebody in Lindside get a grizzly bear hide?" Stella was nothing if not practical.

"I never heard where, from out west, I guess, maybe he went hunting away from here. Anyway, he had this one. It was worn and ratty but he knew no one would get too close to it. He spread it out on the clearing higher up than the blackberry patch and slept in the weak early morning sunshine until the chattering of the women woke him. He put that bear's head on his head and those furry legs on his arms and he started growling. He came down the mountain snorting and snarling, pausing behind trees and bushes until he knew that the women had heard him. Then he ran full speed into that berry patch and scared those poor women half to death. They ran for their lives. Buckets were thrown aside, boots flew off, and as they ran through the briars, their dresses were shredded. Some of them even had their underthings torn off by the blackberry vines. They made it down the mountain half-dressed and bloody from all the scratches."

"What did they do to him?" Stella was hoping he got what he deserved. She was a faithful believer in karma.

"He didn't tell, at least not then. Those women never knew it was him. He didn't tell until most of those women had passed, thirty or forty years later. Said he was afraid to, those ladies would have killed him. They were the very ones who had fed him all those evenings when his wife was gone. He never bummed anymore either."

"What in the Sam Hill was the point of that story, Joey?" Tisha was really more annoyed at the man in the story than the reason for it, but she didn't have him to fuss at.

"I don't know, Tisha, it came to me when Stella fired her pistol and I thought about that poor fellow running through the brush and if any one of those ladies had had a gun, he'd been killed."

Jonas had finished up the garbage bags. "Seems to me it would be an ex-tree-mly bad idea to pretend to be a bear in this field in the next few days." They finished up and hiked back to the farmhouse. The women toasted each other with a bottle of sweet wine in the kitchen while the men talked in the living room. Sunday ended too quickly; tomorrow they would start protecting the trees.

Chapter 25

Tree-sitting

Early Monday morning, Stella and Tisha climbed the ladders up to their respective trees and arranged their spaces, decided they needed more cover for the wind and called Jonas on the fully-charged cell phone. She had promised not to shoot bubbles or do word puzzles on it so the battery would last all day. But this was a supply need, she could call.

"Hey, Honey, could you bring us two tarps and a drill and some screws? We need a windbreak on our platforms. Oh, and some rope, we need to dangle some stuff off the platform to give us more room."

"I can do that after I feed and call in to work. Any sign of the tree-cutters?"

"Nope, but the ram is just standing at the ladder looking up. I couldn't come down if I wanted to. He is a mean old thing."

"Okay, I'll be there in a bit, Tish, all right?"

"Yes, Sir. We finally have time to catch up."

"Good grief, Stella, you could catch up on the phone or in the kitchen."

"Looking at the silver lining, Jonas. It is cold and windy up here, so hurry up."

"10-4, Boss Lady. I'll be there soon."

"Catching up, my eye." Jonas muttered to himself. "Those two are going to get arrested and they are catching up."

Chapter 25

He finished feeding, called Ben, who had already figured Jonas would be out, at the Celanese, then loaded up the four-wheeler with tarps, ropes, a drill with Phillips bits, some matching screws, and a staple gun. By the time he got to the trees, all the sheep were standing around the trees looking up at the tree dwellers. Jonas waded through them and loaded Stella's bucket with a tarp and drill and Tisha's with a tarp and stapler. The sheep pushed each other aside to smell at each new item and Jonas patiently let them smell.

"Where's Eliza today?" Jonas raised his voice under Tisha's platform.

"She says hi, Jonas. I'm on the phone with her. She's at work. We can't both be gone on the same day or Lindside Elementary School will go to the dogs. She'll come tomorrow and I'll go to work." She laughed and turned back to her phone conversation.

Jonas didn't bother to send greetings to Eliza. Whatever they were talking about had Tisha's complete attention. He supervised the construction of a tarp tent on Stella's deer stand and then dealt with her complaint, that she couldn't see in the direction that the tree-cutters were likely to enter the field, by sending up a knife so she could cut a narrow strip in the tarp for a window. When Tisha got off the phone, Stella took over, hollering suggestions for her tarp shelter.

"How many staples are you using, Tish? I thought you were trying to save these trees. Looks like you may staple them to death instead."

"Very funny. Some of the firings of this thing don't shoot a staple. The trees will live," she shouted the last four words so loudly that they echoed. Some of the sheep were startled and began baa-ing.

"I'm out of here." Jonas did not like the sound or smell of the sheep.

The women, only ten feet apart in the trees, chatted a while then took a nap. The sheep wandered off. About eleven o'clock, both women stirred. "Dear God, it feels like I've been up here for days." Tish stretched and rotated her shoulder.

"Four little hours. Wonder when the tree-cutters will come." Stella peered out her narrow window.

"Could be days."

"Are you caving after four hours? Really?"

110

"I need something to do up here, Stella. I know I looked forward to doing absolutely nothing, but I can't do it long. Could we make signs or something?"

"Good idea, I forgot to get an old sheet and paint it. You think about the message we want to write and I'll call Jonas," she answered.

"Jonas, could you look in the upstairs closet and bring an old sheet. Yes, you know the pale blue one I put on the truck seat for Buddy? That would be fine. Uh-huh, top shelf. Oh, and we need some paint. Red and blue and green. Yes. And brushes, small ones. I love you, too." She turned off the cell phone.

"Huh. He sounds a little grumpy." Stella thought about that for a minute. "Tish, let's eat until he gets here. Ham sandwiches, chips, and Dr. Pepper?"

"Sure thing. Are they in my cooler or yours?"

"Yours. Pull that baby up and toss me some food."

After much laughter and betting that the knot wouldn't hold, Tisha reached one hand to the cooler handle and pulled it up onto the platform. She tossed a ham sandwich over to Stella, then a bag of chips, and then a can of pop. They ate in silence until Stella opened her can, which fizzed and erupted. She squealed and threw it down to avoid the pop spray. The sheep came running expecting food and fought over a sip of foaming Dr. Pepper. Then the ram relieved himself long and loud.

"Those sheep are starting to stink." Tisha wrinkled her nose. She loved the fragrance of bleach and not much else.

"Wait 'til ten of them poop under your tree. That really stinks."

"That reminds me, I gotta go."

"You just drank pop two minutes ago."

"What can I say? It goes right through me. Where's the GirlFlo? I've always wanted to pee standing up."

"In the personal items pack. You can use a plastic bag if you don't want to let it fly."

"Nope, that ram was inspirational. I want to do this. And don't watch." Tisha unzipped her jeans and fit the GirlFlo under her. "Here we go. Tim-berrr! Look out below." A stream of liquid arched up then fell and splashed into the early spring grass below. "Oh, my gosh, Stella, I wish I could pee some more. That was fun. Now I see why little boys have contests to see how high they can pee on the bathroom wall at school."

Chapter 25

She removed the GirlFlo and fastened her pants. "Ewww, now how do I clean this thing?"

"Use a disinfecting wipe, Tish. In the personal items pack."

"Now I need that sheet and paint. Where's Jonas? Do we have binoculars, so I can watch for him?"

"Mercy, Tisha Louise, you will be able to hear the four-wheeler for a long way. Read a book or something. It's only been four and a half hours."

Chapter 26

First Skirmish

"Oh, no, Stella. Stella, look."

"You have the binoculars, Tisha, just tell me what you see." Stella was arranging her tree stand so that she could lean against the tree and read. "Quit your grunting, Tish, I'm busy. Just tell me."

Stella froze as a male voice called out. "We're here to cut down the trees. Get out of the way." He fumbled in a clipboard, thumbing through pages. "Akpik, right? I've got the condemnation papers right here." He waved a rattling paper around, which got the attention of the sheep who ran to him expecting sweet feed. Stella looked out the gap in her tarp.

This is it. Confrontation. Don't be nervous. Just take care of business. Before she could get her thoughts together, Tisha found her voice in the next tree.

"Hey, Boy, are you really gonna chop down a tree with a lady in it?" When Stella turned to look, Tisha was standing with her hands on her hips, just like Superwoman. (Stella would later tell that she saw Tisha wearing the whole outfit, cape flying in the wind behind her.)

The man stuffed the clipboard under his arm to control the papers flapping in the wind and pressed a button on his cell phone, all the while pushing noisy sheep away. "We got a problem here. There's two ladies in the trees on the Akpik place. Okay, I'll tell them. Hang on." He looked up.

"Ladies, get out of those trees."

"Is that the best you got?" Tisha remained in her super-heroine pose. "Because if it is, you might as well hike on back and get reinforcements, because we ain't going anywhere."

"Which one of you is Stella Akpik?"

"Over here, Sir." Stella was loosening up. "And what do you go by? You even from around here?"

The man looked her way then put the phone up to his head. "Okay, I asked. Now what?"

"How rude, Boy. I asked you what your name was and where you were from." Stella looked at Tisha. "Must not have had any raising whatsoever."

"Just a second." He turned away from the phone to call out to the women. "Name's Dewayne. Dewayne Wimmer. I'm from Pennsylvania." He went back to the phone. "Okay. Will do. Yep, there's a bunch just over the hill. Yes, Sir, I'll get the crew over there pronto." He hit a button and put the phone in his vest pocket and turned away from the biggest sheep, the ram. "Ladies, I will be back, and I hope you are gone by then." He stared at one, then the other before the ram backed up and lowered his head.

"Move, Boy," Stella shouted. She knew what was coming.

The ram slammed Dewayne's lower back solidly, knocking him forward. The other sheep gathered around the dropped clipboard, tracking mud and sheep manure on the papers as they scattered. He gathered them, limping and staggering.

Stella whispered, "Don't you dare laugh, Tish. Not yet." He walked stiff-legged back through the field without looking back. A few sheep followed a short distance but got distracted and left to nibble on grass.

"Thankee, Dewayne. You just go on home to Pennsylvania." Tisha shouted after him. "I guess he did have manners." Their laughter had a nervous edge.

Stella watched him disappear over the edge of the field. "Why, that wasn't hard," she murmured. *Maybe we can do this.*

"Call Jonas, Stella, quick, before he comes back. No, wait, here comes a four-wheeler." She picked up the binoculars and focused. "They're talking. All nice like. Dewayne's leaving and here comes your big hunk of Eskimo man."

They could hear the four-wheeler and smell the faint gasoline fumes as he pulled up under the tree, sheep parting like the Red Sea.

"We did it, Jonas, we sent him packing." Stella was trembling as she came down the ladder.

"Well, it was mostly me." Tisha struck a pin-up girl pose, one hand behind her head and one hip thrown out to the side.

"Y'all behave," Jonas only had eyes for Stella when he spoke next. "Figured Muttonjeff butted the guy since he was rubbing his back. He was plenty peeved when he left."

"Yep, that ram was magnificent. And if I could reach Tisha to give her a high five I would." She hugged Jonas. "We did it."

"Just a minute, I'm coming down, too." Tisha took her time on the flimsy metal rungs of the tree stand. The women hugged and decided they could spend a few minutes in the tent just to get out of the wind. Tisha dug through the supplies, found tissues and headed for the woods. "Going to the little girls' room," she called over her shoulder, "some things are better outdoors." She disappeared into the trees.

"I can't do that, Jonas." Stella chewed her thumbnail. "I need privacy. Can I go home and go to the bathroom and come back?"

"Nope, but I have you a surprise." He grinned in spite of himself as he uncovered a five-gallon bucket and a toilet seat in the back of the four-wheeler. "Your own, personal, private honey bucket. I'll put it in the barn in the stall where the lambs are born. There's a tarp already around that corner and chemicals, you know, for … "

"I know what for," she interrupted. "If I was a swooning woman, I would be laid out on the ground." She clapped her hands in front of her chin. "That is the best gift ever. Thank you, Jonas."

"I'm off to the barn to install it. Feel free to christen it when you see me heading through the gate." He tipped his John Deere cap and grinned. "Always at your service, Ma'am."

Stella waited until Tisha was back in her tree, singing a twisted version of "I Will Survive," then headed down the hill to the red barn to test drive the new toilet. By the time she returned, the few remaining sheep had ambled away from the trees. It was cooling off even more and Stella grabbed their sleeping bags, tossed one to Tisha and carried hers up to the "tree tent." They rested again before suppertime, then ate and talked until the sunset painted the sky and darkness settled.

"Guess we are going to bed with the chickens tonight?" Tisha sounded like she hoped she was wrong.

Stella yawned. "Yep, I'm beat. What time is Eliza coming in the morning?"

No answer. "Tisha?" A soft snore wafted from Tisha's tree stand. Stella chuckled, *the batteries in the Eveready bunny just ran out.* Then she swished and rustled the synthetic fabric of

Chapter 26

her down sleeping bag until she got comfortable, thought about the day, and slept.

Chapter 27

Another Day in the Trees

The early mist was as thick as pea soup when the women awakened. Stella could hear Tisha's rustling around and moaning as she wriggled out of her sleeping bag and rolled it up before climbing down the ladder.

"Up and at 'em." Tisha whacked Stella's tree with a stick. "Eliza's on the way. She just texted. If I meet her at the road, I have time to go home and get a shower before school." Hearing no answer, she whacked the tree a few more times. "I gotta pee, Stella. I'm going to visit the woods, then head out. See you in the morning."

"What time is it? I'm so sleepy." Stella yawned.

"You might be sleepy because you are freezing to death. Think about that and get your butt up. I'm outta here. Think about me and never-ending bus notes in the office down at the schoolhouse. Have a good day."

"Bye," Stella managed to grunt as she rooted around in the small space to get one more nap before Eliza came.

Stella had slept just long enough to forget where she was when Eliza arrived on the four-wheeler with Jonas. "Look what I picked up hitch-hiking around the mountain."

"Good morning, Sunshine," Eliza chimed in. "We brought breakfast, come on down and eat." Jonas had a box strapped on the back of the vehicle with

two foil-covered plates. He handed one to Eliza. "Looks like cheesy scrambled eggs, bacon, and buttered toast." She finished with her best Grandpa Jones imitation. "Yuuum-Yuuum."

Stella decided it was enough to climb down for and slowly made her way down the ladder. "There's orange juice in the green thermos and cocoa in the silver one," Jonas paused in his explanation. "You okay, Honey? Looking a little rough around the edges." He knew before he finished that he would regret that particular line.

Stella stared at him through mussed grey hair, the seams of her sleeping bag pressed on her face and neck like wide red scars. A crust of dried drool ran from one corner of her mouth, her sweatpants were twisted so that the string was on her hipbone and she was missing a sock. He hurriedly uncovered a plate of food, found a fork, and handed it to her.

"So, what to drink?" She stood frozen in time, processing the comment fully. Eliza was busy eating but peeked to keep an eye on the action. *Jonas is such a good man, but he can say the dumbest things. "A little rough around the edges?"*

"Aww, Honey, you just always look so good in the morning and well, you just don't today." He busied himself getting cups, knowing he had stepped in it a second time. "OJ or cocoa?"

Eliza closed her eyes and twisted her mouth. She did not want to be a witness any longer.

"Jonas Leo Akpik, you know I just spent the night in a tree stand made for … for … " She sputtered trying to find the right word. "Dwarves, tiny little midgets. In a tree, Jonas, in the wind and cold, to save OUR trees, Jonas. While you slept in a warm bed where you could stretch out your legs. And you have the audacity to complain that I don't look good?" Jonas realized she was going to blow.

He took the plate from her gently, re-covered it with the foil lid and put it back in the box. Then he put both arms around her, kissed her on the ear and whispered, "I was just testing you to see if you still had some spirit left to face Mountain Top's chainsaw crew. Glad to see that you still mean business." He planted little kisses all over her hairline and neck. "You are the most beautiful part of my life, and don't you forget it."

She didn't give in without a feeble effort to fuss. "If you ever say that to me again, Jonas, I, I, I don't know what I'll do." He'd picked her up and carried her over to the edge of the woods and stood her up against a tree, his forehead pressed against hers when a scream interrupted them.

"St-e-l-l-a! Come, come quick, here come the MTP men! Run, Stella, hurry!" Eliza was climbing and yelling at the same time. Stella and Jonas took off for the trees and Stella had just made it back up the ladder when a single file line of six green-vested men arrived at the site.

"Good morning, fellas." Jonas stood between them and the trees. "Can I help you?"

"Look, we don't want to hurt anybody, but we need to clear these trees." The man leading the line was older that the others. He had a neat moustache and even in the breeze, Jonas could smell aftershave.

"But these are not your trees, so I reckon you don't get to decide if they are cut down."

The foreman consulted an iPad. "This property has been condemned according to a court decision on March 26 of this year, and MTP needs the trees in the path of the pipeline to be felled in order to begin construction."

Stella said nothing, she was still breathing hard. Jonas said nothing. Eliza called down from the tree, "Oh, Sir, is there anything else you could be doing? Because there are people in these trees."

The foreman sighed. "Ma'am, you can come down on your own or we will bring you down. Both of you." His voice was calm, but there was a new edge in it. He looked around at the workers behind him and renewed his request, "We don't want anyone to get hurt, so come on down right now."

"Seems to me if you didn't want anyone hurt, you wouldn't be building a natural gas pipeline. Last time I checked, gas is pretty flammable and goes boom and kills people. So 'not wanting anyone to get hurt' is another pipe-lie!" Stella's blood was up.

"Lady, I said come down and I meant it." Then to Jonas, "Sir, you appear to be aiding and abetting a criminal action." Jonas shrugged. "So, unless you want to be arrested, you need to vacate the area."

"Don't think so." Jonas crossed his arms.

The foreman turned to the crew. "Call Mountain Top Security to arrest them all."

Jonas cleared his throat, "Your security guys don't have permission to cross our land to get here. Neither do you. MTP promised that all personnel and equipment would be moved via the pipeline path and here you all are walking in across our pasture. We'd like you to leave, Sir."

Chapter 27

The moment was tense. The two men were toe-to-toe, each convinced they were right when shots rang out. Three of them: Bam! Bam! Bam! along with some wild whooping. Jonas hit the ground and green vested men scattered in ten different directions.

"Whoooeee!" Stella yelled from the tree. "I been wanting to do that for a long time."

"I'm half deaf," Eliza whispered and wasn't sure if she was thinking or speaking.

"Stella, if you ever do that again ... especially while I am talking ... or ever." Jonas was dusting the grass and dirt off his knees and elbows.

"Watch 'em run, Jonas. Isn't that the sweetest sight, ever?"

He watched them scale the gate in the distance. "They'll be back. They'll be back with a vengeance, I'm afraid." Jonas spoke aloud, but he was pretty sure he was the only one listening.

Chapter 28

And Then There was One

After lunch Stella hurried to the barn for her toileting needs and scurried back up her tree just in time to hear sirens in the distance growing closer. So did the sheep. They closed ranks, all huddling together in a big circle of animals with the half-grown lambs in the middle. Stella and Eliza watched the flashing blue lights with interest as the sheriff's car wound around Wilson Mill Road at the base of the mountain, getting closer and closer. "Reckon he's coming here?" Stella asked, rearranging her long legs into a cross-legged position. She tucked her hair back behind her ears as she studied the movement of the car.

"Seems likely." Eliza was staring at the same brown vehicle, the blue lights leaving trails in the sunshine, chewing on a fingernail when she decided she better take action and began fumbling in her backpack for her cell phone to call Jonas.

"Look, Liza, here comes Jonas, if he and the sheriff kept going they would crash at the gate." She used her fingers to demonstrate even though Eliza couldn't see her. "Oh, and Jonas is off the four-wheeler now. The police car has stopped at the pasture gate. The sheriff has gotten out. Looks like they are talking. Jonas has his arms folded and the sheriff is waving his hands and pointing up here. Wish I could hear them. Wait, Elmer's getting back in and ... he is turning around! Yay for Jonas!" She clapped, and settled back against the tree trunk to take a bite out of an apple.

"Oh, Honey, bad news, they are coming up Donegal's driveway. I can see them on this side of the hill. The brown police car has three white pickups following it and they are scooting." Eliza's voice was calm, just like her "secretary voice" at work when she managed missing children reports to bus drivers after school. Stella stopped chewing and spit out the chunk of apple she had bitten off. The roar of a speeding four-wheeler coming up the hill had both women peering around their tarps. Jonas pulled up to the trees and turned off the engine quickly.

"Ladies, they have an injunction to keep me 100 feet from their right of way so I am dumping all the food I have in your buckets and clearing out. If you want to end this now, come on down and I'll get you out of here. They plan to arrest both of you."

Both women made their decisions in a heartbeat. "Stella, Honey, I can't miss any more work. I'll send over all my food on the rope between us." The sound of protein bars and pop cans hitting the bottom of a bucket punctuated the conversation. "Pull, Stella, it's loaded. I stuffed my sleeping bag in the top in case you need it."

Jonas raised his voice, "Babe, are you coming down?" The only response was Eliza's footsteps on the metal rungs of her ladder.

After a few seconds, Stella responded, "Why, no, I am not coming down."

Jonas had known her answer before he asked and was implementing a plan while they talked. He'd grabbed a crowbar and a hacksaw from the ATV toolbox and put them in a bucket to be hauled up.

"Separate the ladder from the stand and I'll take it with me. Hurry. I expect they will be coming up the pipeline easement soon."

Stella pulled up the bucket and popped the tree stand ladder loose in two strong prying motions of the crossbar. "Cheap piece of work," she noted.

Jonas gathered up the ladder pieces and put them across the front rack and Eliza crawled on the seat behind him. They headed for the barn.

"Be back soon," he hollered back over his shoulder as he sped away. Then he suddenly spun the vehicle around, throwing Eliza so hard that her leg flew out to the side, and shouted, "And Stella, do NOT shoot that pistol!" He muttered to himself, "I knew she would stay, that woman must be nutty." They raced across the field, bouncing on clumps of grass and scattering the sheep that had been grazing peacefully.

Eliza climbed off at the barn, patted Jonas on the shoulder. "Don't worry Jonas. She is strong and determined to protect y'all's land. When you have pure intentions, what can go wrong?"

"Famous last words, Eliza, famous last words." Jonas did not take his eyes off the tree where Stella sat. "You better get clear of here, get on to the house and get your car and get to work." He broke his concentration long enough to look at Eliza, dusting off her jeans. "Thank you for being Stella's friend. Glad one of you is not going to jail today."

Chapter 29

Security and Deputies

Stella shifted the tarp on the backside of her tree stand to watch the four vehicles approach from the Donegal Farm's driveway. They parked near the proposed pipeline path and started walking. Sheriff Johnson and three deputies dressed in soft grey led the group of Mountain Top security officers, all in brand spanking new black uniforms and tactical gear. By the time they got to the huge oak tree where Stella sat, the creases in their pants were all gone, dust covered their formerly shiny shoes, and if their sweaty necks were any indication, the MTP security crew was regretting their bulletproof vests and backpacks. They were all huffing and puffing except the female captain of the MTP crew; she was stern-faced and cool, even after the hike.

The men stopped under the tree, some wiping their faces and others bent over, hands on knees, trying to recover. After a minute to catch his breath, Sheriff Johnson called up through the newly formed bright green leaves, "Stella, I got a paper to serve. Come down here and get it."

"Elmer, you need to serve a paper to your own boys to stay out of Linda Fox's Hometown Restaurant, look what her donuts have done to them." Stella laughed out loud.

The sheriff waved the folded document above his head. "Now, look here; I have a court order for you to come down the tree, to vacate, right this minute. Stella, do you hear me?"

125

Chapter 29

"Yes, Sir, I hear you, but I can't see those words from up here, so I reckon you haven't served me."

The sheriff turned to his men, his face starting to turn red. After discussing it with his deputies and then with the security team, he made a phone call. He walked away, nodding his head and gesturing with the free hand gripping the folded paper. When he walked back, he was bright red. He yelled up the tree, "Stella, I hope you know you are costing the taxpayers for our time up here dealing with you when we got other things to do."

She shouted back, "Are taxpayers paying Mountain Top Pipeline's employee's too? Uh. I've got better things to do, too, Elmer, but our land is being stolen, STOLEN, by these thugs. And you are helping them. I'm a taxpayer, losing my land, Elmer, I hope you know that."

The sheriff chewed his lip looking at the paper. Then he looked up the tree. He turned and quietly asked the other law enforcement personnel, "Anybody have duct tape?" After a quick search of backpacks, none was found. The newest deputy, Joaquin Guerrero, was assigned the long walk down the hill. His first mission was to find a roll of duct tape.

Meanwhile, Sheriff Johnson directed his men along with the security people to measure a hundred feet from the blue and white streamers that marked the "Limits of Disturbance" of the pipeline easement and put up wide yellow "CAUTION" ribbon. Before they finished, Officer Guerrero handed over a fat roll of duct tape to the sheriff who used it to secure each page of the injunction to Stella's tree. The men finished their measuring and marking and began joking with one another thinking their work was done.

As they began packing up measuring tools, the sheriff called up to Stella, "The injunction is taped to this tree, Stella, so consider yourself served." He chuckled and turned to smile at his followers.

"Oh, no Elmer. I made a phone call, too. My lawyer says if I can't see that paper, you have to read it to me. Not served until you do." The morning birdsong seemed quite loud. "Speak up Sheriff, I can't hear you."

Elmer took off his cap, slapped his thigh with it and stomped off, phone to his ear. The law enforcement men and their female captain stopped their activity and watched him walk away. When he changed direction and started back, they all pretended to be busy adjusting belts and backpacks, watching all the while.

"All right Stella, listen up." Elmer stood under Stella's tree and read the injunction. "It is prohibited to block the legally obtained MTP easement or to be within 100 feet of each outer edge ... "

"Whoa, right there," Stella hollered, " 'legally obtained,' I don't think so."

"Then get a lawyer, this is not a discussion group."

Stella interrupted again. "Got one, Elmer, went to Federal Court, Judge ruled that pipeline companies can steal land."

"Shut up, Stella, I'm trying to read." He continued to read through many interruptions. When he finished, Sheriff Johnson spoke calmly. "You've been served Stella. We will get you down. If you refuse to come down today, we will extract you tomorrow. C'mon boys, we're done here."

Stella whooped and hollered, "Sounds like I'm a tooth, Elmer, extract me, ha, ha."

Again, there was much strapping and adjusting of equipment, paused this time by the sound of an approaching motor. Jonas's red four-wheeler jumped over the edge of the steep approach to the mountaintop field and burst through the yellow tape around the tree where Stella sat.

"Jonas, I told you that you were not allowed within a hundred feet of this easement. Now back off. Now." Jonas didn't move.

The female MTP captain, Kay Balboa, approached the sheriff and whispered, "You can arrest this man now. You have plenty of charges." She paused. "It would be correct protocol, Sir." Balboa had tightly woven braids knotted at the base of her neck just below the black baseball cap. She'd gotten the sheriff's attention earlier. First, because she was a woman, and second because she spent a lot of time stiffly moving between each man whispering to each. *Probably stirring up stuff,* he figured.

"Does your protocol cover me living with these people when you take your big trucks and move on to the next pipeline, Ma'am?" He stared the woman down. She finally turned with military precision and walked away.

Elmer looked next at Jonas who had emptied a pillowcase full of items into Stella's lowered bucket. When he finished and the bucket rose into the branches, Jonas turned. He squared his shoulders and put his hands up. "Don't seem right to be kept off a man's own land." The thick veins on Jonas's neck stood out. Elmer fancied he could see his friend's heartbeat throb in them.

Chapter 29

The sheriff sighed. "Gee whiz, Jonas, put your hands down."

Jonas did so, but his solemn tone was unchanged. "Your goons seem trigger-happy to me." He nodded at the black-garbed group of security, most with a hand on their weapon. "I've seen that look on new public service officers in Alaska when they didn't know what to do."

Elmer addressed Captain Balboa, "Honey, take your crew on down the hill." Jonas flinched, knowing how Stella felt about being called "Honey." Captain Balboa didn't respond. "Oh, that's an order, Missy. You're all done here." When nobody moved, he repeated, "That is an order. My deputies have this situation under control. Go on back."

Glaring, the woman nodded crisply and motioned for the men to fall out. She followed them. Jonas shrugged at the sheriff, "They are all so inexperienced and scared. Be careful that they don't shoot you."

"Jonas, you got to stay away, one hundred feet away. You agreed to that out at the gate this morning. You see what I am dealing with." He wiped his face with a big bandana. "If I had a dog that acted like that woman, I'd get him wormed." He stuffed the bandana in his hip pocket. "Plus, might give him a laxative, too." They chuckled.

"Sorry, Elmer, that was before Stella sent me a list of things she needed." He watched his own feet shuffle in the grass. "I'd rather face you or the magistrate than Stella." He looked up and grinned. "Just leaving now."

Jonas looked up at the tree and raised his voice. "Stella, behave, I'm going on home and mow the grass. Text if you need anything."

"Will do. Don't worry a bit. And Elmer, you and the deputies be careful out there."

"Yes, Ma'am, Miss Stella," a deputy called back as he walked away.

Elmer walked away from the tree with Jonas. "MTP security is going to put guards on her 24/7 at midnight, Jonas. The attempted murder charge was dropped when you told me it was a starter pistol she fired." Neither man attempted eye contact. "Try to talk her into coming down?"

Jonas threw his head back and laughed. "She's nutty enough to stay up there a while, Sheriff, but I have tried and I will keep on trying. I'll put the caution tape back up when I leave. Thanks, Elmer." The men shook hands and parted ways.

Jonas straddled the four-wheeler and reached for the key at the moment Stella called down. "This is important to me, Jonas, don't worry. I love you, you know."

"Yep, I know and I love you, but it's starting to be inconvenient to have a wife who lives in a tree."

"It's the catbird seat, Mr. Akpik. You ought to come up here with me."

"No, thankee anyway. I have chores to do." He tipped his cap to her and backed up the four-wheeler to turn around, headed through the tape, knotted the break together, and headed home.

Chapter 30

I Never Saw a Moor

Stella listened to the big riding lawn mower for a couple of hours in the cool of the evening, wishing she could feel the warmth of her husband's arms. That was the hardest part of this, not touching him. She watched the little Donegal boy feed his hogs and then heard Jonas ride back out to feed the sheep.

He waved at her from the barn, but she knew that he couldn't see her wave back. That act of faith reminded her of a poem she learned in high school. *Who wrote it? A woman, for sure, but which one? That one that carried on with Robert Browning? The tree one that Joyce Kilmer wrote? Wait a minute; Joyce was a boy, wasn't he? The first line is "I never saw ... " something, what? It has been too many years ago.* She thought and thought and finally came up with it and the author, Emily Dickinson. When she got all the lines organized in her head, she softly spoke it towards the barn.

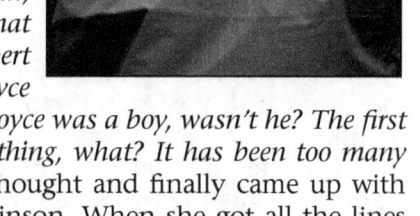

> I never saw a moor;
> I never saw the sea,
> Yet know I how the heather looks
> And what a billow be.
> I never spoke with God,
> Nor visited in heaven.
> Yet certain am I of the spot
> As if the checks were given.

Chapter 30

I never saw a moor or the sea either, Emily Dickinson, and I may not have ever spoke with God, but I believe in Him, too. What a good way to end the day, she thought, *remembering some long-ago poem and seeing Jonas wave at my invisible self. I'll sleep well tonight, probably better than him.*

Stella was right. She slept much better than Jonas did in his lonely bed, worried sick about the guards coming. When he called in to work early the next morning, Ben McDaniel answered and they talked a while.

"Don't you ever let on to Stella that I didn't sleep a wink last night worrying about her. She could fall out of that dang tree in her sleep or when they try to extract her. If she runs her mouth, one of those wet-behind-the-ears security folks may shoot her. I'm going back up and check on her after I feed the dogs and such around here."

"Do you want some company? I kinda hate missing out on the action. This is the news around here." Ben was sincere. "Who would've thought that Stella would be a tree-hugger?"

"Tree-sitter is the proper term, I think," Jonas laughed. "Don't think she hugs the old oak, just sits in it. Look, I better get up there. Sheriff said they'd be guarding her until they extract her. God only knows what she will do."

"Aww, Jonas, I'm coming. This place may have to shut down if we both miss work today, but that's a chance we'll have to take."

"Probably have to close down by noon." The joke was as old as their friendship at every job they'd worked together. "I'll leave the gate unlocked for you."

Jonas did Stella's animal chores, feeding and watering. It took a great deal of self-discipline not to rush up to the top pasture and see what was going on. The dog fairly danced, the cat arched her back and rubbed his leg, and the chickens gathered at his toes to be fed. Every animal that approached him seemed to expect a pat on the head and an extra bit of food. He filled a bucket with sweet feed to take with him to the sheep. *Stella has probably spoiled them, too,* he thought.

By the time he got out to the gate, Ben's truck was sitting there inside the field. When he saw Jonas, he pulled over and jumped out to get the gate for him. Jonas parked the four-wheeler and brought the bucket of feed.

"If you'll take me by the barn, I'll let out the sheep and we can go up together."

Ben nodded.

When they topped the hill, they found a white tent under the oak and two black-uniformed security guards in place, both looking upwards through the branches.

"Stella, you okay?" Jonas's voice boomed from across the yellow tape.

"Yeah, I'm fine. The neighborhood is going downhill though. Thugs have moved in. Can you see them?"

"Yep. Ben's with me, too."

"Hey Stella, how's life in the tree this morning?" Ben was grinning ear to ear at the young guards, who were marching over to the men.

"Doing good, Ben. Try to keep my sweet baby outta trouble down there while I am away, will you?"

"Yes, Ma'am, will do."

"Excuse me, Sir, you both have to leave, you can't be here." The guards looked even younger as they got closer, thin chested, lanky young men, breathing hard and talking fast.

"Why's that?" Jonas lowered his eyebrows.

"This is a restricted area, you can't be talking to the protestor. There is an injunction. It's on that there tree." The young man pointed at the oak.

"Well, Son, I believe that means my body can't go over there, but my voice surely can." He looked at Ben and rolled his eyes when the guard turned away to confer with his partner.

"We can allow you to talk, but don't take one more step, not one."

"Is he fricking kidding me?" Ben searched Jonas's eyes.

"I'm telling you, these folks are untrained and inexperienced. MTP has hired every 18-year-old in the area that ever shot a gun, pays them $37 an hour, dresses them like soldiers and puts them in the field."

"Good God, there is going to be bloodshed on this project. Theirs, from mishandling their guns," Ben added.

"Look at these two right now," Jonas nodded toward them and Ben could see both had hands on their holsters.

"Boy," Jonas spoke firmly, "when is the extraction attempt?"

"This evening, Sir, if she doesn't come down on her own before then." The second guard called him back and spoke with him. The first guard continued, "Sir, that is confidential information. Do not share it."

Jonas and Ben exchanged looks. "Reckon he knows he just shared it with the ones that the information is most important to?" Ben chuckled.

Chapter 30

Jonas shouted, "Y'all have a good day, hear? You, too, Stella."

"Bye, Baby," rang from the tree.

"Get in the truck, Ben, my phone just buzzed with a text. Probably Stella."

They pulled themselves up into the cab and closed the truck doors. "Oh, great, just great. Here's her text." He reached his phone over to Ben.

> I am staying until they drag me out, Honey. Here for the long haul. The longer I block this pipeline, the more money it costs MTP and the better the chance of bankrupting them. Love you.
> P.S. Kinda feel sorry for the security boys. Don't you two mistreat them. But have at that woman. She's so mean, she probably argues with fence posts.

Chapter 31

About Ready to Sing

Naomi sighed as she stared at the ceiling, sleepless once again. When insomnia hit, she usually preferred to think about the future, but tonight was different. This night she reminisced about her childhood, the shanty near Pence Springs, West Virginia, where she had been so lonely for so many years. A scooped-out space in the dirt under a small evergreen tree had been her favorite spot. There, she could watch the comings and goings on the road in front of the house and not be seen.

Lying in her spotless room seventy years later, she could still smell the dirt and the pine needles. During her earliest years, there were few times when anyone looked for her or called for her to come out. Screaming fights, broken beer bottles, and little or no money led her to her hiding place often. Her mother ignored her, busy with other things to do,

especially after her daddy left. By the time she was ten, she was left at the poor house hoping for foster care.

She was rescued by the Rutherfords, who adopted her as a playmate and maid to her new foster brother, Pennington Alexander Rutherford, crippled by polio. His name was a mouthful, and she had shortened it to Penny. Naomi never held his status of older, blood-related child against him; she loved him dearly. From their first meeting at the family's mansion, a big, rambling Victorian farmhouse outside of town, her main sources of joy were her foster brother and the secrets they shared. He was her cheerleader and protector until she left home at seventeen to marry handsome Randall.

The troubled home that she escaped plus the violent end of her troubled first marriage colored her behavior forever. Ashamed to go back to the foster home, she lived in a shabby apartment in Hinton and made a living as a call girl for years. She had no regrets about her life; she believed that she had done what had to be done. Penny rescued her again after his parents died, and they had a business partnership now. For many years, she had been unhappy, but now, with enough money to do as she pleased and enough education and experience to lead others around to her way of thinking, she was content.

One of her greatest pleasures was the sport of courtship. Luring men in by a variety of wiles, being needy for example, or by throwing money at them, was such fun. When their attention waned, she simply salvaged what she could, including their worldly goods, and set them free. She curled into a ball in her luxurious sheets, remembering the men she had done away with. Like a flash of lightning, the memory of the end of her first marriage crossed her mental eye.

Randall had been a handsome man who smiled and gently held her hand in public, but in private committed physical atrocities to her tiny body. She smiled all these years later, recalling the look in his eyes when he saw that she was serious about him leaving. Self-defense, the lawyers said, and the jury agreed. She had realized her power when he fell to the ground. The jury's decision was just the icing on that particular cake. She stretched, yawned, and then curled up again. Finally, sleep came.

Early the next morning, she studied her face at the lighted dressing table mirror and pushed her cheeks upward over and over with moisturized fingers. *Maybe the time had come for a lift.* She drummed her perfect nails on the tabletop. *No, life is just too busy right now. Maybe later.*

Jonathan was picking her up at nine o'clock to go to the lawyer's office. The survivorship papers had been drawn up for them to sign. She didn't know how long she would dally with Jonathan, but that stupid brand had hurt and the uniqueness of his cruelty piqued her interest. She thought he might be deserving of her skills.

Today, after they finished at her Myrtle Beach lawyer's office, she hoped to motor on down to Charleston. *I want a piece of coconut cake from that darling Peninsula Grill in the historic part of downtown. Jonathan will choke when he gets the bill. Last time I was there, a slice of cake was $12 and the entire 12-layer cake cost $130.* She giggled to think of that wonderful dessert and of Jonathan not knowing what it would cost. *Hmm, if he doesn't fall apart at the Peninsula, maybe we can tour downtown in a horse drawn carriage.*

She corrected the part in her thin hair and applied her makeup carefully, especially around her eyes and lips. *I don't have to look so pitiful any more, but the damn wrinkles keep multiplying,* she thought as she used concealer and foundation. A last look in the mirror, *not too bad,* she thought, then turned off the mirror and went to dress.

By 8:45 she was seated out at the front door where chirps from a small aviary drew her attention away from the window. She watched the tiny finches often, but there was clearly a ruckus going on in there this morning. The cleaning lady joined her and Naomi asked, "What in the world is going on in there?"

"That's the new boy in town." She pointed to a red-beaked bird singing his heart out. "And he is looking for a new baby mama."

"Do the females sing back?" Naomi was very interested and not a little surprised that the cleaning lady knew so much about finch behavior.

"No, Ma'am, only the boys sing. The zebra finches are supposed to be monogamous, too, so that will slow him down. They should've put a new girl in there at the same time." They both stared at the tiny courtesan. "But, I think this young lady steps out on her fella," she said as she pointed to a quiet orange-beaked bird, "because I've seen her with two different males."

"Fascinating." Naomi studied the drama until she heard the front door open and looked up. There was Jonathan, looking at his watch before breaking into a smile when he noticed her.

"Looks like he's about ready to sing hisself." The cleaning lady nudged Naomi and picked up her bucket.

Chapter 31

"Good morning, Dearest." Jonathan opened the nursing home door for her then stepped lively around her to open the car's passenger door.

"Was that woman talking about me?" Jonathan asked when they were both buckled up. "What did she mean?"

Naomi patted his hand. "She just meant that you were a dapper young man and had the world by the tail." The new facts about finch behavior delighted her, but she wanted to roll them around in her head before she talked about them.

"Guess it's time to see that lawyer of yours." He slid his hand out from under hers as though he needed it to turn the steering wheel. Naomi knew better.

"What's his address?" Jonathan's tone was one of a man in a good mood.

Naomi smiled. "My lawyer is a she, Jonathan. Her name is Susan Solomon."

"Ah, the power of traditional thinking. I assumed the attorney for such a lovely client would be a man." He stole a glance at her while driving.

"Head north on 17 Business, her office is just off the highway on Twenty-First Avenue North." After a pause, she continued, "I think you will like her. She is a no-nonsense woman and she's had nearly 50 years of experience in estate planning. Be sure to ask her anything on your mind."

Jonathan wondered aloud, "Hmm, not sure I know enough to ask anything." Inwardly, he fretted, *the questions I have are not going to be asked today. Will catch her later, without you, my sweet.*

Once he put aside the fear that his true identity was in danger, the two hours spent in the old-fashioned law office were quite satisfying to Jonathan. He yearned to touch the heavy velvet drapes, and rubbed the cool, polished cherry arms of his chair when he thought no one was looking. The floor to ceiling shelves lined with law books impressed him, as did Ms. Solomon. She had to be at least 80 years old and sat at a massive dark cherry desk with reading glasses perched on her nose. Her explanation of the documents was so detailed that Jonathan drifted away from time to time, imagining what this lady's home must be like. He entertained thoughts of wooing her, but decided to look her up after Naomi, when he had more money to work with.

As he was poised with the pen over the signature line, he asked, "Could you just review the basics for me one more time?"

in an effort to impress both women with his thoroughness. He didn't notice that they both stifled smiles; they'd been acquainted since Naomi's working days.

"Yes, Sir, basically, when either of you die, the other party will inherit the entire estate of the deceased, all assets and all debts." She turned to face Jonathan more directly and took off her glasses, "There is a considerable age difference in play here, so we assume that you will be the survivor, Mr. Wesley. This is Mrs. Waterman's tangible commitment to you. If something should happen to you prior to her death, she will enjoy the same rights of survivorship."

Jonathan nodded and began to sign, then stopped short again. "And how does the power of attorney work?"

The attorney smiled patiently, "This authorizes you to engage in specified business, financial and legal transactions on Naomi's behalf. It is called 'durable' because it does not terminate if she were to become disabled or incapacitated. It gives Naomi the same authorization over your affairs."

He grinned broadly and signed with a big capital J and even bigger capital W. He helped Naomi up and to the desk so she could sign. The papers were notarized, which required Jonathan to produce a photo ID. He had expected to be asked and dug a fake driver's license out of his wallet, courtesy of a forger friend of the prostitutes that had once attended his church.

His future had just gotten a lot rosier. After they shook hands and made arrangements for them both to get copies of the newly-signed contracts, Naomi meekly asked, "I'm so happy to have that morbid business taken care of. Let's grab lunch somewhere close, then would you have the time to go down to Charleston this afternoon and celebrate with a piece of cake?"

"Anything in the world for you, Sweetheart," he swung her hand as they walked to the car. If Jonathan had been physically able to jump up and click his heels together, he would've.

Chapter 32

Naomi & Margaret

The nursing home hallways were quiet when Naomi arrived home late that night. Jonathan dropped her at the front door. She used the handrail every few steps to steady her tired legs. The nurses' station was empty, but she found the clipboard and signed in. When she passed Margaret's room, the door was open and she could see a warm glow from a floor lamp surrounding her friend who was reading in a rocking chair. Naomi was drawn to the scene and tapped weakly on the doorframe. Margaret looked up.

"Well, good, you are back. Come on in, come in." Margaret turned her paperback book face down and escorted Naomi to the rocker. "Sit down right here." She smoothed the cushioned seat and patted it.

"Thank you." Naomi settled in lightly, like a little bird. "What did I miss around here today?"

"Same ole, same ole." Margaret sat on the side of her bed sporting flamingo-patterned pajamas. She leaned forward, "The real question is, how did **your** day go, Missy?" She pointed at Naomi, who had laid her head back on the head cushion of the chair and was smiling.

"Jonathan and I got some legal matters taken care of." She giggled. "Men are so trusting, aren't they?"

Margaret's eyebrows went skyward. "You didn't marry him, did you?"

"Oh, no. He hasn't asked – yet, that is." She snuggled into the oversized wooden rocker and chuckled. "But he will."

"Oh, good Lord, Naomi. What do you need with a husband? You have what you need: a nice home, friends, a parade of

141

Chapter 32

online shopping deliveries, AND a boyfriend that drives you around." Her tone turned more serious, "You've been married before, haven't you?"

In answer, Naomi held up her arthritic hand and spread her fingers apart, her body shaking with laughter.

"What? Five times? Where are they all?" Margaret was on the edge of the bed now.

"Well." Naomi coughed gently and covered her mouth with her hand. "Let's just say they didn't work out." She closed her eyes and relaxed for a moment, then peeked to gauge Margaret's reaction. A lifetime of secrets had disciplined her conversations and she was wary. She saw Margaret's twisted forehead and mouth on the verge of a smile and was satisfied that her words had at least been interesting. She waited for Margaret to speak, but there was only the buzzing of the hallway lights.

"Cat got your tongue?" Naomi opened one eye and grinned.

"I'm not speechless very often, Girl, but this one takes the cake. Do you have any children, any family?"

Naomi hesitated. She'd not talked about her past with anyone at the home, but she was just so tired and wanted to open up a bit more. After squinting at Margaret up and down, she decided to trust her. "Just one brother. He lives at our home place in West Virginia, manages the place, you know. I miss him." With that, she fell asleep.

Margaret watched her sleep, stunned at her revelations. She shut the door and went to check that Naomi had signed in. *They'll read her the riot act if she didn't,* she thought. Satisfied that her guest was properly documented, Margaret now had to get her to her room next door. She did so by waking Naomi enough to get her to her feet and supporting her as she shuffled to her room.

She helped her undress down to her bra and panties and pulled a gown over her head and arms. She adjusted it and tucked her in the bed, but not before she'd studied an ugly heart-shaped burn on her bony, wrinkled chest. "Oh, boy," she whispered, "What have we here? J.W.? Oh my God."

Margaret looked both ways when she left Naomi's room, closed the door softly behind her and returned to her room. She tossed her book aside and crawled into bed. She had some serious thinking to do.

First, I won't tell Nurse Danvers a thing. Penny is probably her brother's name, but I'll keep that little tidbit a secret for now. I already got his address from Danvers. Next, married five times? I only knew about two, just heard rumors about others. Maybe she is innocent and maybe she is lying. What happened to all of them? Clearly Jonathan is looking for a Sugar Mama, not a wife. Is he responsible for that heart-shaped burn scar? I will report that to Nurse Danvers and she must report to law enforcement. That is elder abuse. Unless Naomi had agreed to it. Dear God.

Daybreak found Margaret twisted in her sheets, her pillow pounded out of shape. She hurried to dress and go to breakfast early in order to keep up with Naomi.

Meanwhile, Naomi was dressing herself leisurely, wondering why she hadn't taken off her lacy bra for bed, but shrugged it off concluding she was just too sleepy the night before to tend to herself properly. She remembered Margaret's help only in bits and pieces.

When she strolled into the dining hall for breakfast, there was a committee of vultures waiting at her table. Much like rowdy high school cheerleaders teasing one of their own in the school cafeteria, they spoke loudly enough for her to hear, teasing her.

"Wonder what time someone got home last night?"

"That same someone is positively glowing. Hmm. Wonder what she's been doing?"

Then crudely, "Tell, tell, did your ticket get punched, Naomi?"

"Now, be nice, girls. Naomi will tell us what she wants us to know." Rosemary then addressed the celebrity, "Honey, sit with us and tell us all about your day yesterday. You lead such an exciting life, compared to us homebodies."

Naomi did glow then, in the spotlight of her friends' attention and admiration. "Let me get something to eat, girls, then we may talk."

She could hear them buzzing as she selected her foods and motioned for a kitchen helper to carry her tray to the table. During that time, her friends reorganized to leave an empty chair in the middle of the group and pulled it out for her. She sat down regally, a queen with her subjects, and fed them little crumbs of information, not the least of which was a description of her piece of yesterday's coconut cake.

Margaret was suspicious. *Naomi is too happy. Is this a normal relationship, even for the elderly?* Then she answered herself. *No, something is very wrong and I am going to find out what it is.*

Chapter 33

Down Time

Stella made it eleven days in the tree before she came down. She watched heavy equipment move in on either side of her and rip up the sod and dig through the topsoil. She heard the workers joking about her and watched them leave each evening in their personal pick-up trucks, all licensed in faraway states: Texas, Oklahoma, Arkansas, Missouri, and the like. Her affection for the tree grew, and once she had worked through her anger at the situation and accepted the strong likelihood that she could not save it forever, she was at peace. Years later, when others spoke of her days in the tree, she only smiled, the absolute peace she'd felt was her secret.

The cherry picker had arrived during the first week and the deputies rode it up to extract her. She simply ignored them and they couldn't bear to force her down. Some of the deputies agreed with her stand.

They came down and told the sheriff that they were afraid someone was going to get hurt. Sheriff

Chapter 33

Johnson was very angry with them all, including the deputies and Stella, but he lashed out most at MTP Security Captain Balboa. She'd suggested that his men were lacking discipline and needed training. Elmer told her what she could do and where she could put that training. If he could have thought of a reason, he would have arrested her.

Supplies had run out a few days before she came down and there had been no rain to replenish her water supply. Jonas and Ben had tried to shoot her sandwiches using a potato gun over the guards' heads. They had gotten a teenager to use his drone to deliver one power bar, but their efforts were mostly unsuccessful.

In her efforts to help, Captain Balboa held up a wrapped cheeseburger to show Stella, then laid it on the ground and told her, "All you have to do is come down and get it." Stella immediately poured the contents of her makeshift honey bucket on Captain Balboa's head.

"Oops," Stella had said.

The Monroe County judge had eventually ordered her down and levied a fine of a thousand dollars per day for as long as she stayed in the tree beyond the eleventh day. She'd further negotiated with the sheriff that if she came down according to the court order, he would not arrest her for trespassing. MTP Security Captain Balboa was furious.

But mostly the reason she came down was that Jonas asked her to. He'd texted her a sweet message of support every day, but on the eleventh, he broke. "Worried," he wrote, "Will do anything you want for as long as you want, but your days up there are days I can't be with you. Please come down." That's all it took.

She texted back, "Bring the tall ladder first thing in the morning and tell Tisha and Eliza to call the press. I love this old tree but I love you more."

And that was that. Stella was trembling on the ladder and hungry, but she was okay. The TV station from Bluefield was there and several reporters wanted to talk to her, but Jonas waved them away.

"Jonas, I think I can talk. Be a pity to waste a chance to tell why I was up there." She looked at him with tired eyes and he motioned the WVVA cameraman and reporter to her. Other reporters followed, anxious for a story after their hot dusty walk up the hill. The WVVA reporter handed her a microphone.

146

"Well, I just wanted to tell you good people what possessed me to climb that beautiful tree and sit in it." She paused, her mouth dry. "Ain't it a shame? I don't have enough spit to tell y'all. But if I had any extra spit, I'd use it on them." She pointed at Captain Balboa, who wisely ducked her head, only showing her austere plaited hairstyle. "Yep, her, the one with the power braids, who comes in here, like all of them, from away somewhere else and tries to enforce court orders to suit her greedy, pipeline employer on the backs of our land and water. This pipeline is no good, people." There was a rousing cry of support from the crowd. "No good for us or for Mother Earth." Stella coughed and Jonas looked askance. She nodded her head. She was okay and ready to go on.

"Jesus Christ wouldn't want us to treat the land this way." The crowd got noisy again with scattered "Amens." "Good farmers wouldn't treat the land this way. People who care about the future don't want this. Will grandchildren and great-grandchildren have water, will they be able to use this beautiful land?"

She swept the view from the high field with her arm. "I say we defend our land, whatever the cost may be, fight them in the pasture fields, fight them in the courts, fight in the mountains and in the wetlands and from our rivers they want to destroy. Fight the judges who live in the pockets of the oil and gas industry." She was red-faced and shaking her fist in the air, a picture that was used on the front page of the Monroe Watchman that next week, when she ended, "Never surrender. Protect what you love!

"And the banks and politicians that WE elected, they are not on our side. Whose side are they on?"

The crowd answered, "MTP, MTP!"

"We don't even get to use this gas." She shook her head, "No! Do you know where it is going?" The people didn't say a word; just waited to hear. "To the ports at Norfolk to go overseas, to who knows where? Our land was taken so the foreigners can have gas. Are they going to get blown to smithereens when there is a pipeline explosion here?"

"Nooo!" The crowd responded.

"Are they going to lose pristine water from springs and wells?"

"Nooo!" The crowd answered. It was taking on the ambiance of a tent revival.

"You're not going to stop us," an MTP worker dared to express his opinion as he sat at the wheel of a bulldozer.

Stella unleashed on him, yelling, "You ever heard of David and Goliath? Probably not," she laughed. "I'll tell you how it ended – the little guy won."

The crowd cheered. "Anybody remember the one Chinese guy who stood up to a bunch of tanks?" The crowd cheered. She whispered aside to Jonas, "Did he get killed?" Jonas shrugged. She went on, "And I don't know what happened to him, but the picture of his bravery was pretty amazing.

"You young men working for MTP, you be careful. This terrain is so steep and dangerous; they have budgeted for 18 deaths of workers during this construction." The crowd grew quiet. "MTP thinks you are expendable, Sir." She pointed at the man on the bulldozer. "I am talking to you, Sir. Stay safe."

Jonas watched as she struggled to clear her throat, then took her upper arm, "Time to go?" his eyes asked. She put up one finger.

Taking a deep breath and gulping a slug of water from the bottle Tisha offered her, she went on, "Gerald O'Hara knew what was important. He said 'Land, Katie Scarlett. Land is the only thing worth fighting for, worth dying for.' We must protect our land and water." She held the water bottle high. "Cheers to the power of the people! I gotta go home now and rest. Keep fighting, all you people!"

The crowd cheered as Jonas led her away. The cameraman walked beside them to the truck, where Jonas stood behind her to hoist her up if needed. She pulled herself in, rolled down the window and waved as they headed home. He spoke when they headed downhill.

"Nice speech. What's first on your list of things to do?"

"Thanks. I think a hot shower is first." She finished the bottle of water.

"Good, you smell pretty rank." He grinned.

"Jonas, I have had my own natural gas for three days and nowhere to go to escape it. Bugs have eaten me alive. I have peed and pooped in a bucket. My hygiene needs some work, yes, but my heart is full to breaking. I have done what I can do to stop the pipeline bastards."

He looked at her, "Really?"

"Well, for today, anyway."

Chapter 34

Sleepover Preparations

Naomi's hand fluttered more than usual as she dabbed a tissue at the accumulating drool from the wrinkle at the corner of her mouth. Her dressing table mirror reflected a perfectly fitting turquoise outfit, subtle yet effective makeup, and every white hair in place. She was ready for some action and expected it to be very difficult for Jonathan to refuse. She'd reserved a private cottage at the Ritz Hotel right on the ocean. It was rated five-star and should be nice enough to entice Jonathan to appreciate his surroundings.

She tried to imagine what she'd overlooked. Nothing, she concluded. She'd arranged for champagne and strawberries to be delivered to the cottage after dinner, had a new silky short gown, used moisturizer for face and body and nether regions, and was carrying a variety of fruity gels and edible massage oils.

Still she worried. *There is nothing left to chance tonight. My main worry is his wandering eye. He is starting to look at other women.* She'd noticed him looking at bikini-clad girls from the pier while he thought she was sleeping. *The way he looked at Susan at the law office wasn't good either. I've dealt with this sort of behavior before. I must nip it in the bud. A private cottage will be good for our first night together. I'll have him all to myself.*

One more glance in the mirror, a wiry curl had sprung loose. She exhaled and noted to herself, *I just hate what the years have done to my hair. No conditioning treatment on earth will change this brittle stuff back to the lush hair I once had.* She tucked it back behind her ear, added final spritzes of perfume behind her ears, on both wrists, and one at her midsection. Smiling, she imagined Jonathan being close enough to notice

Chapter 34

the flowery scent. She was ready. Steadying herself, she stood, picked up the sweater and purse on the bed, carried them in one hand and extended the handle on her wheeled suitcase with the other. She began the walk to the nurses' station to sign out. Margaret caught up with her in the hall.

"You look lovely. Hot date?"

"Thank you." She pursed her lips. "Can you keep a secret?"

"I am a vault." Margaret bobbed her head up and down like a salesman pitching a product.

"Jonathan and I are spending the night together." She blushed prettily and added, "I suppose someone here should know."

"Well, how about that." Margaret seemed thrilled. "His place?"

"No, we have a cottage at the Ritz. Number Five, I believe." She pulled a reservation paper from her purse. "Yes, Number Five it is."

"Do you have a phone?"

"Yes, Ma'am. Right here in my purse. Before you ask, I have your number already on it."

"Well, you have fun, but not too much." Margaret smiled.

Naomi nodded and walked the gauntlet, past the card game table to the nurses' station to sign out. The table of women got noisy.

"Wooo, look at Naomi, looking fine."

Sweet Teeny managed a thumbs up and another serious compliment, "You look divine, Naomi." Naomi nodded to her.

"Bet Jonathan's gonna mess those clothes up." One of the ladies cackled and got the group going.

"Use it or lose it, Baby." They pounded on the table and cheered their girl on which led to the appearance of Nurse Danvers.

"What do we have here?" The sturdy nurse looked Naomi up and down. "And where do you think you are going?"

Naomi drew herself up to her full height of five feet no inches, "It is perfectly ridiculous for a woman of my age to have to account for my whereabouts, simply ridiculous." She nervously adjusted the sweater folded over her arm.

"You better sign out and list a phone number." The nurse's tone was all business.

"Tell her to blow it out her ear, Naomi, she's jealous."

One of the new residents began singing, "Na-o-mi's getting some, Na-o-mi's getting some, Na-o-mi's getting some."

"You ladies sound like a bunch of construction workers." Naomi turned, hiding her smile as she signed out. The women continued chanting until they all collapsed in laughter.

Danvers walked away muttering, "Mean little girls in old ladies' bodies."

Naomi waved as she pulled her wheelie towards the front door amid kissing sounds and cries of passion from her friends.

Margaret pulled out a deck of cards, ever ready in her pocket, took her seat at the table, and prepared to deal to the spirited group of women. But her thoughts were swirling around Naomi's plan for a big night.

* * * * *

Jonathan was still waiting for the copy of his power of attorney contract. He'd tried to transfer money from her checking account to his, but the lady at the First National Bank of Peterstown was firm in denying the request until the bank had a hard copy of the agreement. He'd called the lawyer's office to find out what was causing the delay, but Ms. Solomon wasn't ever in and promises to have her return his call hadn't been kept. He was frustrated and could feel that his emotional merry-go-round of "anger, fight, get over it" starting up again.

He only used the room in the back of the chapel to sleep and change clothes. He cruised the boulevard in the Cadillac when he was not with Naomi or singing at Sea View. He endured the odor of sweaty socks and decaying food as he began to straighten up his tiny living space, swatting the flies that had moved in with the smell. He looked around the room. A layer of sand covered the floor and spiders worked in the corners of the windows. His makeshift desk was covered with price tags and department store receipts. Dirty clothes were strewn over the folding chair and fast food wrappers overflowed the cardboard box he used for a trash can.

Jonathan counseled himself. *If I can just hang on a few more weeks and get the power of attorney thing recognized by the banks, I am going to be able to pile up some money fast. I'll be set for life. The car will be mine. Her house will be mine.* As he counted his chickens before they hatched, it occurred to him that he had no idea about her real estate holdings. *Did she even own a home? Need to ask about that.*

Only his new purchases brought him comfort. He gave up on cleaning up the mess to choose one of several new shirts for tonight's outing. He'd bought pajamas, new underwear, and a small expensive suitcase for the event. That item cheered him

151

most, reminding him that his days of packing in a grocery bag were over.

Jonathan was painfully aware of Naomi's expectations for the night and shrugged nervously. *I can't do this*, he held his head in his hands. I can't even stand to touch her skin. A bottle of bourbon and a girlie magazine had been his original plan to get through the evening, but he hadn't really believed this would ever happen.

His last attempt at intimacy was with a woman he picked up in front of the Pavilion who had flashed her breasts at him. She was feisty and drunk, an inviting target, and he had wheedled an invitation back to her hotel room. He learned quickly that she was trying to make her boyfriend jealous and that he was on the way. Jonathan exited down the stairs before the boyfriend showed up, her laughter ringing in the stairwell.

His church services now consisted of lectures to stray people about their evil ways. He had all but quit preparing sermons. It was getting harder each week to even show up on Sunday mornings, but surprisingly, a few people always straggled in. He resented them showing up. His anger built when he had no choice but to use some of his stipend from Naomi to supplement the pitiful offerings to pay the chapel insurance. He had to have a place to live, no matter how terrible. The more immediate problem, spending the night with Naomi, was the priority at the moment.

How would he get out of this nightmare? He remembered the plump, smooth skin of his long-ago wife, Alice, and the excitement of touching her with burning cigarettes and how she had screamed. Just remembering excited him. *Maybe save that for later; Naomi might pass out. Yes. Brilliant.* He snapped his fingers. *She needs to pass out beforehand. Sleeping pills. What is the name of that date rape drug?* He quickly searched the internet on his phone and found the name, Special K or ketamine, and rushed downtown to find a junkie with a contact.

Proud of his cleverness, he found who he needed in a seedy alley behind a bar and the young man convinced him he didn't need Special K, he needed sleeping pills. So, he got both. He was ready for tonight, anger forgotten. The next morning, he would brag on her about how good she was and how much he enjoyed her body. He pounded the steering wheel with glee and promised himself it would all be worth it in the long run.

Chapter 35

Vacation Time

Stella awakened slowly, contentedly, without opening her eyes, knowing it was morning by the light through her eyelids and the sounds of the birds. They sounded farther away, almost muffled, than they had the last eleven mornings. She stretched, moaning happily until her toes touched the end of the bed.

She heard the bedroom door creak and rolled over. "Breakfast in bed, M' Lady." Jonas was carrying a cookie sheet with dishes on it.

Scooting up in the bed, she made delighted sounds, "Ah! Oh, how thoughtful, you shouldn't have," until she saw the plate. One protein bar, unwrapped and centered on the good china. Jonas laughed and laughed as he stepped back into the hallway to get another plate piled with biscuits and gravy, butter melting in little pools, scrambled eggs with orange bits of shredded cheese peeking out of the mound, and three perfect sausage links.

"I wish I could've had a video of your face falling." He pulled a chair over to sit by her while she ate.

"Cruel, Jonas, just plain cruel." She spoke with her mouth full of eggs.

"Are you okay?"

"Yeah, why are you asking?"

"I don't know, Hon, last night, you know, when we, you know." His eyes questioned hers.

Stella thought, her fork poised in the air. "Oh, that." The fork found its target and she chewed before she spoke. "It was hard to concentrate on having a good time when my leg was

153

Chapter 35

cramping. Oh, I guess I was just stove up from sitting in the tree. You've had cramps before at 'inopportune' times, too, Jonas. Remember when you had to get up and hop around and put hot towels on your calf. That was pretty funny." She resumed eating.

"Yeah, guess you're right," he nodded. "I had forgotten about that. Easy to forget pain in the middle of things, I guess. So, do we need to get bananas or potassium pills or something?" Jonas shifted his weight in the chair and scratched his head.

"I don't think so. Probably just need to use my leg muscles. Last night was a good start, Babe. Maybe we can invent a new exercise program for tree-sitters." She looked up from her plate and winked. "They'll just have to find a new exercise partner."

"Good. No other ill effects from the tree adventure?"

"Not unless you count bug bites and sunburn. Millions of bugs must live in that tree."

"So, are you okay upstairs?"

"Mentally, you mean?"

"Yeah, Stella, you've been pretty angry or tense or something. What with the pipeline and our trees and stuff. You okay?"

Stella took her time, chewed slowly, and said, "I got rid of a lot of it in that tree. There was a lot of time for thinking up there. I got everything thought out from Timmy Lee and Daddy's death up to these greedy pipeline companies. I even thought about God and dying and said some prayers for us all, except maybe for the asshole security woman. I probably won't ever be completely over her." She grinned. "I trust her lousy karma will catch up with her."

She gazed out the window at the blue sky meeting the green trees of high summer. "I know there is still anger deep down, but right now, at this minute at least, I am okay. I've done all I know how to do." She reached for Jonas's hand.

"Good. But when the trees fall and the heavy machinery moves in, can you handle that?"

"I honestly don't know." She wiped the napkin over her mouth and laid it on her empty plate. "Guess I will fight it day by day."

"That's what I want to talk to you about." Jonas cleared he throat.

"Oh, Lordy, must be serious." She tried to get a clue from his face but there was nothing there.

154

"I talked to Ben. I have nearly a hundred vacation days built up, well, minus the fifteen or so that I've used here lately. I could use them to fund insurance after retirement or I can use them now."

"Spit it out, Jonas. I'm nervous."

He inhaled and spoke all in one breath, "I think we should forget about the garden this summer, get someone to tend to the animals, someone to cut the hay, lock up the house, and get out of town. Anywhere you want to go."

Stella's jaw dropped, thoughts racing madly through her mind like a laser light show. Then she knew. "I never saw the sea." She first spoke softly and mechanically as if she were reading, then met his eyes and spoke up, "I want to see the ocean, Jonas." She paused. "And not the Arctic Ocean either, I want to see the one with white beaches and lazy waves and sunshine. Myrtle Beach. I want to go to Myrtle Beach." She reached for him with both hands and he pulled her out of bed into his arms, dishes clattering, then rolling onto the covers.

"I love you Jonas Akpik," she whispered into his beard.

He grunted, "Kinda sweet on you, myself."

"Well, time's a-wasting, we have work to do. Leaving you in the house as a bachelor for almost two weeks has left its mark. I need to clean and wash clothes and Lord knows what all."

"I'll get out of your way and go pick up cat feed and dog feed and sweet feed so the animals are stocked up for Ben to feed while we are gone. Look around and tell me what we need from town."

Stella gathered up the dishes and stacked them on the make-shift tray. "Here, take these to the kitchen while I spread up the bed and get dressed. Let me check the refrigerator and see what we need. Do we take food with us or eat out every meal?" She hopped around putting on clean underwear while Jonas watched in amusement. "That can't be good for us or our pocketbook. Better pack food. When do we leave?"

"Looks like we'll be ready in about an hour at this rate." Jonas cleared his throat. "I need time to mow the grass one more time and talk to Ben about exactly what needs to be done. Probably need to change the oil in the truck, too, and get the hay in. How about first of the month?"

She had pulled on a shirt and shorts by then and hugged him, cookie sheet and all then danced away, singing, "We're going to the beach!" The truth was that she had wanted

155

to leave that very hour, but the anticipation was almost as exciting as leaving so she was happy to wait a few weeks.

"Didn't know you'd get this worked up. After you settle down and get your stuff done, go online and see if you can find us a room or something for a week or two." He stopped in the doorway. "I hate to be away from you at all, but I need to get some things done to make this all happen, so I'm gonna go feed then take your list to town."

"Feed? Oh Lordy, Jonas, I am half crazy, I forgot my poor animals. I'll go feed, right now. I need to tell them we are leaving but we'll be back."

He chuckled and gazed at her, visibly happy that she was home, then switched gears. "Okay, I'll load up the dishwasher and run it. Ben and me aren't much for washing dishes." He had been concerned that she might disrupt the pipeline work in the field and was relieved that the trip would be a distraction. He bounded happily down the stairs.

Stella threw herself on the unmade bed and spoke to no one in particular, "I can just barely believe it. At sixty years old, I am finally going to see the Atlantic Ocean."

Chapter 36

Ritz Number Five

If a little birdie had been watching the Ritz on the Shore in Myrtle Beach, Cottage Number Five, that night, and could speak about the activities there, strange would've been a word used in the description. An elderly lady and her much younger escort arrived hand in hand, laughing as he fumbled with the key. Dinner arrived from room service. The man left and returned with a pair of swim trunks in hand. While he was gone, the woman came outside and made a phone call. The man returned hours later. Another woman arrived and hid behind the nearby sand dune for a while, then scurried to a spot under the cottage window and sat for hours in the dark. She left. The man ran out, banging the door open. He paced in the sand and angrily kicked the pilings of the cottage foundation.

As streaks of pink colored the sky at dawn, he sat on the deck alone, slumped and motionless. He finally went inside. Two police officers knocked on the door before breakfast. The man motioned them inside. They went inside, and then left. Breakfast for two arrived. The man left and returned just before noon. The same man escorted the woman out  at midday. She appeared to be much feebler than when she entered the evening before.

* * * * *

Jonathan returned Naomi to the Sea View Nursing Home and uncharacteristically walked her to her room. Nurse

Chapter 36

Danvers blocked their path in the hallway, linebacker-like, both hands on her hips and shoulders squared.

"How are we this afternoon?" She emphasized **afternoon.**

"Naomi has a headache," Jonathan said. "We had a late night."

"Humph, I just bet you did." She turned her attention to Naomi and softened her voice, "Hon, are you okay?"

Naomi nodded and smiled.

"I'll take her from here, Reverend." Her voice expressed contempt for his title and behavior.

Jonathan did not hesitate. Wordlessly, he handed off Naomi and her wheeled bag, and headed back towards the front door.

"Good riddance," Danvers muttered. "Now, Miz Waterman, let's get you to your room and maybe some liquids and a nap?"

* * * * *

Jonathan drove home in a rage. Somebody had reported that a person was in danger and sent the cops to the cottage. *Who else knew about them being there?* He hadn't told, for sure, and he doubted Naomi had. Things had been going so well, friendly and nice and he had been able to kiss her warmly and hold her in his arms and she was happy and appreciative. Then she'd wanted to swim and he didn't have swimwear. *Who would've thought the old lady would want to swim?*

He left to buy trunks, but the busy boardwalk distracted him. Firm young women, souped-up cars, and guys throwing away handfuls of money at the shops held his attention for longer than he realized. The anger had returned. He didn't have any of those things, and the only way he saw to get them was through Naomi. He'd rushed out of her slow world of pastels, the sickeningly sweet fragrance of peonies and trembling hands and had no desire to return. Eventually, greed won that particular internal battle, and jaw clenched, he'd stomped back to the cottage, intent on his mission.

He found her seated in the bed, dressed in a thin negligee and sipping champagne when he returned. All his attempts at an explanation for his delay in returning were waved aside.

"All that is really important is that you are here now." She giggled. "I started without you, Dear. Pour yourself one." Naomi motioned with her glass to the bottle.

"I believe I will. Here, let me refresh yours while I'm at it."

He knew he should thank his lucky stars that the deal could still be done. Back turned, he emptied a Special K capsule into her drink, then for good measure a half of a capsule of the sleeping pill. Alert about mixing the glasses up, he was again relieved. Hers had the imprint of pink lipstick on the rim. Smiling, he turned back to the bed, handed her the drink and sat his down to undress. Twenty minutes later, she was out like a light. He'd provided her with lots of love and attention and he hoped she would remember.

He dressed and watched her breathing. Then a horrible realization hit him. *You idiot, this is the perfect time to finish her off. No one knows we are here. But you can't, can you? The power of attorney paper hasn't reached that one-horse bank in Peterstown. Damn. Damn. Damn. This could've been over.*

As if in response to his thoughts, she mumbled in her sleep. *I could kill her with the pillow right now. The paperwork would be straightened out eventually.* His greed for long-term security spoke as loudly as his desperation to be free of her. Clutching his head with both hands like a madman, he ran out the door.

Jonathan didn't realize it, but, like most people, movement tranquilized him. He walked and kicked and punched the air until exhausted, then collapsed in the deck chair at the cottage. He stared at the cracks in the deck flooring and the grains of sand there until he had the happy thought that maybe he used too much of the drug and she had died on her own. He went inside to check.

She hadn't moved and his heart raced with excitement. He watched for breathing and saw none. *Now, what? Do I have a little mirror I can put under her nose and see if there is any breath?* He did not. In lieu of that dubious test of life, he felt her scrawny neck for a pulse. *Damn it all. Her heart is beating. Slow but steady.* He sat down on the bed tired and disappointed. *I'll just stretch out beside her for a minute. Maybe catch a nap and clear my head.*

He was sleeping soundly when the pounding on the door finally woke him. He tried to speak and no words came. He cleared his throat and tried again. "No room service right now."

"Myrtle Beach Police. Open the door please." The voice boomed and he all but fainted.

Jonathan looked at Naomi, had she died? No, she was breathing. "Just a second, I'm coming."

He answered the door, hoping he looked like he'd been sleeping, which he had, but he ruffled his hair with one hand in case.

"This is a wellness check, Sir. We got a report that a person was in danger here. Could we come in?"

Chapter 36

Jonathan could not speak. He held open the door and motioned for them to enter. They interviewed him briefly, checked his ID and stood in the bedroom door, watching Naomi sleep.

"Sorry to have bothered you, Mr. Wesley. Have a nice day." The officer tipped his hat and was gone before Jonathan could process the "what-ifs" or think how to show his outrage.

Another knock on the door nearly paralyzed him with fear. Breakfast had arrived and he set the tray inside.

He couldn't stand the cottage another second, and burst out again to the beach where he walked and walked, picking up shells and greeting early risers. He calmed down and headed back to the cottage to wake Naomi up and get her back to the nursing home. He'd had enough for now.

Chapter 37

Packing

"Jonas Akpik, do you even own short pants?" Stella called across the hall where Jonas was changing from grass-covered jeans. He'd just mowed. She'd designated the big guest room bed as the staging site for packing. There were piles of clothes and towels and two open duffle bags covering the bed.

"Can you let a guy get his pants on? I'll be there in a minute."

Stella had washed up all the clothes and then decided to wash their bed sheets, and then she could see that the room needed to be dusted and vacuumed and then the windows needed washing and if she was going to clean the bedroom, she might as well clean the downstairs rooms. In the kitchen, she reorganized the cupboards and wiped them out before scrubbing the floor. Consequently, she was a day behind in getting ready to go to the beach. She chewed a nail as she surveyed the current mess.

"Are we leaving anything at home?" Jonas had joined her and put a hand on her shoulder. "You are taking this way too seriously. Let me show you." He scooped up a pile of his clothes and dumped them in the duffle bag and zipped it up. "There, I'm ready to go."

"What if they get wrinkled? What if you don't have enough socks or underwear? Will you need button-up shirts?" She was unzipping his duffle when he spun her around.

"I hear tell they have washing machines in South Carolina. And if we need something, they have stores, too. Relax."

"Oh, Jonas, how am I going to relax when I don't know what to expect and how to get ready for it?" He held her tightly against his chest.

161

Chapter 37

"Whatever you do is okay. If we have too much stuff packed, it is okay. If we don't have enough stuff, it is okay. Do we have a room, by the way?"

"No, I can find them on the computer and I can fill out all the stuff to make a reservation but then I get scared that it isn't a good place and lose my nerve and don't finish."

"It is all okay. We can grab a room when we get there. Probably better off to see it first anyway."

"What if there aren't any more empty rooms?"

"Then, we'll drive away from the beach until we find one and look again the next day."

Stella was sorting through the piles of clothes. "Do you have shorts?"

"Don't remember ever having any except for gym class or to play ball in. Do you have a bikini?" He didn't smile, just looked at her like it was a serious question.

"Oh you," she swung a tee shirt that she was refolding towards his head like a weapon and he ducked and laughed. "Be a cold day you-know-where when I wear a bikini out in public. Oh, that reminds me, we are going to burn our fish belly pale bodies, let's get some sunscreen. Do they make 100 SPF?"

"Hello, my arms are brown."

She pulled up his pants leg and drew his arm down to his leg. "Your uppers don't match your lowers. I am going to make you some shorts before we leave. Where are my good scissors?" She straightened up, "Are you going to wear boots at the beach? You have boots and you have sneakers. Do you have sandals or flip flops?" She covered her mouth to hide her smile. She knew that was ridiculous.

"Stella, have you ever seen me wearing flip-flops? Did you like my pink ones with the rhinestone flowers between my toes?" He grinned and she laughed out loud, then moved on to another concern.

"I just don't know. These towels are a little bit ratty. Can we use towels from the motel?"

Jonas ignored her. "I'm going to go up to Bob's; the refrigerator is plum empty. What do you want for lunch?"

"Surprise me." She was focused on the mounds of clothes again.

Jonas stomped down the stairs whistling. Buddy hobbled up to meet him at the back door and Jonas talked to the dog in baby talk while he patted him, "No, Buddy-Boy, you are not going to the beach, your wittle paws will burn up. Big ole

Ben will take good care of you while we are gone. You watch out for Stella's sheep, you hear, and keep those mean coyotes away. Yes, I will watch out for your mamma while we are gone and try to keep her out of big ole twouble." He laughed and walked on to the truck.

Through the open upstairs window, Stella had heard the one-sided conversation and it nearly took her breath away. She instinctively reached for her heart, partly because of the pure sweetness of it all and partly because she just realized that Buddy would be here alone. Timmy Lee could come and burn down their house. And there was still the pipeline. She could hear the buzzing of chain saws in the sheep field this morning and the beeps of heavy equipment. Maybe she didn't want to go to the beach after all.

She sat on the bed and thought about it a while, then decided she needed a good slap on the side of the head. Buddy would be fine, Timmy Lee was long gone, she had done all she could to stop the pipeline, and she was going to see the ocean!

* * * * *

They left with the back seat of the truck full of coolers and boxes of food, pots, and pans. Jonas had mentioned there might be a place with a kitchen. He regretted it immediately, but Stella did not want to "haveta buy somethin' we already have." The bed of the truck held their duffle bags, some fold up chairs they borrowed from Ben, a tent, "in case all the rooms are full," sleeping bags, and some firewood if they had to camp out. Jonas responded to Stella's question, "You reckon the sheets and pillows in a motel will be clean?" with a shrug, so a garbage bag of flat and fitted sheets and two pillows with clean pillowcases were added to the load. By then, Jonas had given up and only asked her to tell him when she was finished so he could put the tarp over the bed in case of rain. She went back once to pet Buddy and to be sure the cat had enough food. Buddy retreated to the shade under the deck steps and Stella was satisfied that the dog would survive without her. She smacked the truck fender twice, her signal that it was time to go and pulled herself up into the front passenger seat.

"Are you sure you are ready?" Jonas teased.

She punched him on the arm. "Let's go south, big man. Eat some seafood, dance on the boardwalk, and play in the waves. I been hearing tell about Myrtle Beach all my natural born life." She broke into a decent version of "On the Road

Again" and Jonas sang with her, bumping happily along the mountain road all the way to the paved Route 219.

Stella read the road signs with a big atlas on her lap, her finger on their approximate location. "Oh, let's stop at Fancy Gap, Tisha buys flowers for the cemetery at an outlet store there. Turn off at Exit 9." She measured the distance on the map with her knuckle. "Not far, about ten miles."

"No problem, Ma'am. We made it an hour and a half without a stop. Better than I figured we'd do."

They left with two big bags of artificial flowers for the grave of Stella's friend, Anna, and gifts for Eliza and Tisha for "tree-sitting for the great and glorious cause."

As Jonas unstrapped the tarp, he noted, "There is a limit to the space in this truck, just in case you forgot."

They made it to the foot of Fancy Gap Mountain, Stella oohing and aahing at the view of Pilot Mountain in the distance before she needed a bathroom break. "Never been to the bathroom in North Carolina," she laughed as she slammed the truck door.

Jonas pressed on the GPS app of his phone while she was gone and checked the route and estimated time of arrival. *Looks like suppertime at the beach,* he figured. *No sense in showing this to Stella, she's having such a good time navigating.*

Stella opening the door surprised him and she saw the map on his phone. "What's that?" She pointed to the colorful screen.

"It's a computerized map. It can figure the route and the distances and tell you where you are."

"Well, I'll be. How does it keep up with all the new roads? Wait a minute, are you saying you don't need me and my atlas?"

"No, no, not at all."

"You can't look at it while you drive. I guess it can't talk to you like I can."

Stella reassured herself for just a moment before a British girl's voice spoke, "Return to the route. Return to the route."

She looked at Jonas, "You have another woman. When were you going to tell me?" They laughed. Stella grabbed her map book, "It's on. Me against your British robot woman. I'll be a modern-day John Henry, mental strength against the machine." She looked at Jonas. "You can choose which one of us to listen to." He shook his head. This was going to be an interesting trip.

Chapter 38

Amazing Atlantic

By the time they crossed over the South Carolina line, Stella had called the computerized GPS voice "your little British witch" so often that Jonas had pulled over and turned his phone off. Stella had claimed victory and sang "I am the Champion" until they looked for a place to eat.

By mid-afternoon they were in downtown Myrtle Beach and Jonas pulled into a parking lot. "Get out, girl. It's show time."

Stella stepped onto the pavement, stretched her stiff legs, and looked around. Gift shops and blinking neon signs surrounded her. "This must be what New York City looks like," she said, spinning around to take it all in. He took her hand and led her to a wooden sidewalk through the sand.

Chapter 38

"Close your eyes. No peeking." He led her through a cut in the sand dunes out onto the hard-packed sand. She heard it before she opened her eyes, the pounding of the waves and the swish of the water spreading and receding. She tuned out the noise of the people on the beach and their radios and clutched Jonas's upper arm. He led her to the water's edge. "Now, Baby. Open your eyes."

She was so quiet that he had to get in front of her to look at her face. "You okay?" He laughed. "Is it what you expected?"

Her eyes never wavered. "It goes on forever and forever. I didn't know it was so big." She turned suddenly. "It feels like we can't go any further. We've reached the end of the earth, the end of land." She stood watching the waves. "It never stops. Always moving."

Jonas took off his boots and rolled up his jeans and nudged her. "Might as well get in it. They say salt water cures everything."

Stella joined him and they put their shoes and socks high on the beach away from the water. "Won't somebody take them?" Stella looked at all the people.

"Nah, probably safe as can be." He took her hand and they ran splashing into the water skimming over the sand, venturing out to the baby waves, then walking along the beach for a long way.

"When the tide goes out, we can come back and look for shells," Jonas explained.

"Can we just stay on the beach and watch the water all night? I don't want to ever leave."

"Well, we need to get a room and a bite to eat. Then, we can come back, I promise." They found their shoes and Stella hugged him.

"Thank you," she whispered, "I had no idea how it would feel to be here. Everything is soft. The air. The water. The constant movement. I couldn't feel it just looking at pictures."

They carried their shoes back to the pavement where they quickly realized the need for them and slipped them back on.

They cruised Ocean Boulevard southward. Stella, forgetting about the need for a room or food, just looked at the sights. People were packed on the sidewalks and traffic moved slowly. Several miles later, Jonas pulled over. "I have an idea, let's get out of the touristy area and go on down to Garden City Beach, just a little ways down Route 17. It's not as crowded and it is a lot quieter."

"Same ocean?" Stella was serious.

"Exact same one."

"Yes, that's a good idea. I liked looking at all those blinking lights and watching all the people, but I didn't want to be in the middle of them." She shivered. "Can we come back up and look around, maybe go in the gift shops?"

"Sure thing, Baby, but let's see if there's a condo with our name on it at Garden City and then some food." She nodded happily.

He pulled out and found the 17 Bypass and picked up speed. In a few minutes, he pulled up at Dunes Realty where they found an available one-bedroom condo on the beach just a few blocks away.

After lugging the duffle bags up the stairs and shoving them through the door, Stella ran to the front of the unit and held back the long drapes over the sliding glass doors. "Look, Jonas, it is right here, all the power and," she stumbled for a word, "all the big-ness of the ocean."

Her wonder was contagious. Jonas stood by her, reflecting on the size of the world and the divinity that created it, feeling very small.

"Makes me think of God and how big He must be." Stella spoke as if she had sensed his thoughts. Jonas nodded.

"Let's go eat." Stella turned and walked briskly to the door, stepping over their luggage. "I'm hungry and you must be, too."

Chapter 39

Take Me Home

Jonathan was chewing his fingernails as he drove along the ocean. He was feeling hemmed in. The taste of money and the status of driving the Cadillac had persuaded him to take Naomi here and there, to talk several times a day by phone, and to play the role of boyfriend, or whatever he was, but he had to end it. Soon. He needed to be free yet still keep the money and the car and whatever else she had. The power of attorney was official and he had transferred a little money just to test the system. It had shown up in his account last night. It was time to talk to her, to do something. He pounded the steering wheel

Chapter 39

with the heels of both hands, then turned around and headed to Sea View Nursing Home.

He parked, plastered on a smile, and headed into the facility, thoughts scrambled; he had no plan in place, just anger eating at him because he had to continue this farce.

"Good morning." He knew his charm wasn't going to work on Nurse Danvers. She grunted at him as they passed in the hall.

Thankfully, there were no others in the path from the front door to Naomi's room. He tapped gently and listened at her door, then pushed it open a few inches. "Good morning, Dear."

Naomi was seated at her dressing table, brushing her hair. She was nearly ready for the day. "Hello. Aren't you the early bird, darling. Are you after the worm?" She laughed and resumed brushing. He didn't know what to think of that.

"If you are the worm, then yes, indeed." He kissed her on the back of her neck and looked at her in the mirror.

"We are a handsome couple," she patted his cheek as she spoke. "Jonathan, Honey, we need to talk."

She turned around and patted the bed for him to sit down, which he promptly did, curiosity tempering his anger. "Jonathan, I've got to go away for a few days. There is a legal issue at the farm, back home in West Virginia."

"Can I help? I can go with you." His plan started to form. "I can drive you, Naomi."

"But you can't miss a Sunday, and I will be gone over one or two Sundays." She fumbled to find an earring in her lap and put it on.

"I can get a lay speaker to cover for me," he replied, while thinking *or put a "Gone Fishing" sign on the door.*

"Jonathan, I don't want to come between you and your calling. Are you sure?"

He started breathing easier. "No problem at all. We are in this together, Naomi. What's the legal issue?"

She folded her hands. "A pipeline has been built through the home place." She noticed his frown. "Oh, we were well compensated. Very well. But now, there are issues with our water supply. Since the blasting, one well has gone completely dry and a number of springs on the mountain are yielding very little water."

"Can't you handle it here? There are ways to sign papers electronically, E-signatures, I think they call it."

"No, my darling. I must go. The caretaker, my brother, Penny, needs my presence and advice. He has asked me to come."

"When do we leave?"

"Can you be ready by morning?"

And not have to sit here or take you somewhere in slow motion or listen to your phone conversations or touch you? Yes, Ma'am. He spoke, "Absolutely, but I can't spend time here today. I'll need to make some arrangements to be gone."

"Of course. Then pick me up at, say, eight in the morning?" He nodded and made his escape. *I am just her driver,* he thought, *she didn't even thank me. But, with benefits, financial benefits.* He hurried to the car. *A day off!*

Naomi waited for several minutes, plenty of time for him to be in the car and gone. There was no rush. She found her cell phone and pressed a number. The party on the other end answered on the first ring. "Hello," Naomi spoke softly. "It worked like a charm. We are all set." She hung up and sprayed a new fragrance in the air to sample it.

Chapter 40

Stella Sees Him

After a few days of absorbing the novelty of life at the beach, Stella and Jonas fell into a comfortable routine. Mornings and evenings were spent outdoors, and during the hot hours in-between, they stayed inside; cooked and ate in the condo or went shopping, although Stella's shopping enthusiasm waned after two days. By the end of the week, they still had a list of things they wanted to do. Jonas had fished from the pier a time or two but wanted to go deep-sea fishing. Stella had found a shell tour she wanted to go on. She wasn't ready to face pipeline construction at home just yet so they made arrangements to stay another week.

Stella was still mesmerized by the ocean but she wandered inland from time to time. She felt confident enough to drive the truck around, at least to the Garden City Grocery and out to the pizza place for pick-up. This particular morning, she dropped Jonas off at the dock at Murrells Inlet to go fishing and stopped at a red light on the way back to the condo.

A cream-colored Cadillac pulled up right beside her on her right, and she glanced absent-mindedly at the man driving and froze. She looked back up at the light before it changed and, unbelieving, looked again at him. It was an older, more stylish version of Timmy Lee; silver hair cut neatly, wearing a lavender knit polo shirt.

She searched his hands on the steering wheel for confirmation. As if in answer to her question, he moved his right hand across his chest to scratch his left shoulder and there it was, or wasn't. She could see the shortened finger, the top joint gone, left in shop class at Briarcliff High School in Atlanta.

173

Chapter 40

The light changed and the Cadillac moved away. She was conscious of the car horns honking behind her before she stepped on the gas to move forward. Her no-good, murderer of a brother right here in Myrtle Beach. Fighting the urge to run and hide, she did the opposite, gunning the engine and changing lanes to follow him. She could see him three cars ahead, still in the right lane. Finally, she got directly behind him and recited his license plate number aloud over and over, singing it to keep it in her memory, 8OL-915.

She followed him for miles, all the way back to Myrtle Beach. Her mouth was dry, but she could feel the sweat trickling down her spine. He turned right and the light changed to red and she was stuck watching him go down the street. That gave her time to feel for a pen in the console and write down his number on her hand, shouting it in rhythm as she wrote. She moved forward and took the next right to circle the block and try to catch him, but he was gone. Quickly, she pulled into the back parking lot of a Taco Bell, threw open the door and vomited. It was early, so no customers were watching. *Probably not the first time someone had thrown up in a fast food lot,* she thought.

She called Jonas. No answer. *Probably no signal out on the Gulf Stream, wherever that is. Should I call Sheriff Johnson? Probably. He could at least run the license and get an address.* Fingers shaking, she dialed the Monroe County Sheriff's Department. No answer. *Too early,* she looked at her watch and sighed.

She spit in the grass to get rid of the bad taste and headed back to the condo to pull the covers over her head and think.

Stella got turned around on the way back, but eventually saw familiar landmarks and the place they were staying. She rushed upstairs, stripped off her clothes and pulled on her flannel pajamas, threw herself back in the bed, and pulled the comforter over her head. There she lay for an hour, doing something she had vowed never to do again: reliving every horrible thing Timmy Lee had done to her and to others. Her own rapid breathing scared her and she tried to relax. Then she came alive. "No!" she shouted. "Not again. You are not going to control me or cause panic attacks. Never again." She threw the covers back and sat up, yelling, "Look out, you rotten, no-good, murdering, disgusting excuse for a man. I am done hiding from you or worrying about you!" With a flourish of bed linens, Stella stood, looked skyward, fists clenched, "As

God is my witness, I am coming for you, Timmy Lee Davis, and I won't stop until I find you."

She found her phone and speed-dialed Jonas. The call went straight to voice mail. She hung up, thinking, *nothing he can do from a boat at sea, anyway.* Quickly, she found Sheriff Johnson's contact information and pressed his number.

"Good morning, Stella."

"Hey, Elmer."

"Thought y'all were on vacation."

"We are, but I need a favor. I need to find out about a car down here. I need the license plate numbers run." She held her breath waiting for an answer.

"Does this have anything to do with the pipeline? Those boys are still pretty sore that I didn't arrest you out of that tree."

"No, Elmer, but I sure thank you for letting me go. Jonas is grateful, too. We owe you, that's for sure."

"Are you in some other kinda trouble down south? Tell you what, let me speak to Jonas."

"He is deep sea fishing today and besides, he don't know anything about this."

Elmer let that sink in. "Generally, we like to know why we are sending in license plate numbers, Stella; not just because somebody, not even in law enforcement, wants to know."

"Elmer, I am begging you to get me a name and address for this car owner. It may be nothing and it may be something, but I figure I am saving the Sheriff's department a ton of money by checking it out."

"Well, we are out a ton of money from last month with the overtime you caused in that tree." Stella thought it best not to comment. "But, it looks like MTP is going to pay the extra money. The County Commissioners have sent them a bill." Then he paused. "Oh, shucks, this is about Timmy Lee, isn't it? Stella, he is a dangerous man. Let me call the Sheriff's office down there and get them on it. You shouldn't be messing around with him."

Stella spoke calmly; she knew Elmer tended to stay calmer if those around him were calm. "Might be him, might not be. Get me the owner's name and address and I'll find out. If he is at all involved, I will call you back. I promise."

Elmer breathed a long deep sigh. "I will probably regret this, but okay. One of the boys will text you the information."

"Thank you, Elmer, thank you."

Chapter 40

"And you stay clear if it is him. That's an order."

"Yes, Sir, I will be so very careful. Elmer? Elmer? Are you there?" She looked at the phone, no sound or other sign of life. "Why, he hung up on me," she spoke aloud then threw that thought aside and scrambled through the tourist brochures and magazines in the living room for one with a map of Myrtle Beach. "Look out, Timmy Lee, I am hot after you." She found a couple of maps, fixed a piece of buttered toast that she could hardly chew, and waited.

Within ten minutes, her phone buzzed and a text appeared. Naomi R. Waterman, 219 Middleburg Drive, Myrtle Beach, SC. 29579

It pained her to wait for even one second, but she took time before she ran for the truck to text the sender back, THANK YOU!

Chapter 41

Lost and Found

Stella was lost. She had thrown the useless maps in the floor of the truck and pulled over to try the map thing on her phone. She typed in the address and a blue flashing dot appeared on the screen with a street map. A voice spoke, "Turn right in 50 feet." She followed the other directions to the address and learned that she had "reached her destination."

She drove through the parking lot, looking at the building. *This can't be right, this is an old folks' home.* She looked at the text again and the address on the sign. They matched. She stomped inside and lost some of her steam when she saw the elderly residents finishing up breakfast. *This can't be right.*

She stopped at the desk and asked if Timmy Lee Davis worked there, but the receptionist had never heard of him. She lingered in the hallway, looking out the window, watching birds in the aviary, reading the bulletin boards. Then she saw him, at least his picture. She read the notice for a sing-along twice, then ripped it down, stuffed it in her pocket, and hurried to the truck with it. Proof. She HAD seen him. He was here, in this town, maybe in this very building.

* * * * *

She sat in the truck, stewing. Jonas wasn't due back until after dark, probably ten o'clock. It was going to be a long day waiting for him, but she needed help.

What is Timmy Lee doing driving a Cadillac that likely belongs to a resident of a nursing home? How can that evil man pass for a preacher? Could he have changed? She laughed bitterly at that thought. *Should I call Elmer back? I did agree to. No, I'll wait for Jonas. What have I become, lazy in my old age? What do I*

177

need Jonas for, anyway? She made up her mind to act alone and marched back into the facility.

"Excuse me, Ma'am. Does a Naomi Waterman live here?" Stella was leaning over the counter trying to read upside down any papers lying around there.

"I can't give you that information, we are not allowed."

Stella was stumped, then she remembered the notice in her pocket. "Can you tell me if the preacher … " The word stuck in her throat, " … the man that leads the sing-along, is he here today?"

"Oh, Reverend Wesley?" Stella nodded, her fingers going numb. "Why, he was here, but you just missed him. He and Mrs. Waterman left for an outing not 15 minutes ago." She realized her mistake. "Oops, I shouldn't have said that."

"Did they say where they were going?"

"Not to me, but I bet Margaret knows. Let me page her. Have a seat right over there."

Stella allowed herself to breathe. A tall woman with regal bearing visited with the receptionist, who motioned towards Stella. The woman approached her and extended a hand. "Good morning, I'm Margaret and I know Reverend Wesley. Can I help you?"

Stella realized at this point that she was in her pajamas with uncombed hair and toast crumbs Lord knew where. She shook hands and tried to smile and not act as deranged as she probably looked. "I was hoping to see Reverend Wesley. There's a problem, a family problem, and I need to find him. Do you know where he went?"

Margaret studied her. "I don't know exactly where, wait, I do have a possible address, but he is going to be gone several days."

Stella flopped back in the chair, hand to chin. "Look, I really do need to find him. It is very important. He's not what he seems."

Margaret looked puzzled for only a second, then her forehead smoothed out. "Would you like to talk about it?" When Stella nodded, Margaret stood. "Let's find a quieter spot. Come with me."

Chapter 42

Country Roads, Take Me Home

Naomi slept most of the long trip from South Carolina to West Virginia. Climate control in the car helped keep them both comfortable, and Jonathan was especially enjoying the cool air blowing up his back from the air conditioners in the seats. He was swaying to the music as he listened to Gospel Gold, his favorite Sirius radio channel. He happily sang along, telling himself, *this will be over soon Timmy, my boy, and you will be out of her clutches forever.*

He hoped that the farm was located way out in the country, someplace where accidents could happen without anyone seeing or hearing a thing. Penny was a wild card, but if he was an older brother, he must be ancient. He reminded himself he was close to Stella's stomping grounds. He had to lay low, get the job done and move on somewhere else.

The roads got narrower as they approached West Virginia. The Oceanside Interstate changed from an eight-lane divided highway to a four-lane to two-way traffic on a two-lane road. Now they were on a paved strip, a back road without enough space for two cars to pass one another on the

road; one of them had to run along the gravel shoulder of the road.

The sound of gravel crunching woke Naomi and she wiped her mouth and got a tiny sip of water from a bottle. "I see we are almost home, Dear. Only a few more miles from here."

Jonathan hoped the farm was closer than that. He worried that the road would get worse. He was glad to see the remoteness of their destination, but his nerves were on edge as he fought to miss oncoming vehicles in curves.

"Taking your half in the middle, are you, Jonathan?" Naomi was reviving, laughing and pointing out sights that she remembered. "There's a cave up through those woods, there. I ran away from home once and slept in the cave."

"What happened?"

"I went home the next morning. I really don't think anyone missed me but Penny. I told him the whole story many times over the years, the shadows of the bats got bigger every time I told it." She giggled like a little girl, caught up in being near home. "And there is a tree in a curve I hit the first time I tried to drive off the farm. I wonder if there is still a scrape on it. Of course, it was a lot thinner then, just a sapling. That was so very long ago." She cut her eyes at the driver as if she was assessing his attentiveness before speaking again in a more serious tone. "I do hope you like Penny. He doesn't get out much, but he runs the farm very well. This new pipeline has been a terrible problem from the get-go. It is up and running now, they say, but water tables have dropped or disappeared and people are in danger of losing our water sources all along its path."

Jonathan growled, "How many acres do we, I mean you and Penny, own?" Something about his tone reminded her of his poor reaction when she first told him about Penny. *He wants absolute control,* she realized.

She straightened her seat belt. "At this farm, about 400."

"Are there other farms?"

"Oh, yes, but we have people overseeing them. One in Greenbrier County and one in Summers County and then, I have some agricultural properties in North Carolina."

Jonathan whistled. "That's a lot of land. I had no idea." He gripped the wheel tighter and tried not to smile.

"All right, now Jonathan, when you see a stone column on the right," she pointed, "with a sign on it that says 'Rutherford's,' turn there."

"Whatever you say."

Naomi leaned forward to watch and soon pointed and shouted, "Right there. There it is." Jonathan saw nothing but stones covered with vines. As he turned he could see an empty bracket for a sign and what might've been a board lying flat on the ground.

"Looks like the wind got it," he tried to help her save face, but she didn't seem bothered. *I bet this place is a wreck,* he thought as he picked his way carefully up the rough road, straddling the biggest ruts, huge gullies from run-off. The road was lined with trees, some connecting overhead to form a green canopy of sorts.

"Careful, Dear. Penny has certainly neglected to have road work done."

He slowed and made his way as safely as he could, avoiding larger rock outcroppings and holes. Finally, around a curve, the jungle of hardwood trees opened up and he could see an old-fashioned farmhouse sitting on a knoll. It needed paint. A classic example of the last century's Queen Anne's home, it had an intricate roofline with three eaves each facing different directions. A huge, rounded front porch wrapped around the lower level, complete with rocking chairs in a row and potted Boston ferns swinging from the front edge of the ceiling.

Jonathan pulled up as close as he dared to the front steps. He didn't get out fast enough to help Naomi who was out and up the steps in a flash, calling, "Penny, Penny, oh, Penny, I'm home!" She opened the outer screen door and called inside, "Penny, we're here."

Jonathan heard a scraping and a squealing before he saw anyone and then a small form filled the door. It was a man with a strong-looking upper body and withered legs. He walked with two metal hand crutches.

Naomi hugged him face-to-face, they kissed each other's cheeks and he patted her gently. "Little Naomi, it is so good that you came home, it's been too long." He looked at Jonathan, "Is this your latest?" Penny grinned an elfin smile as if he didn't care if he was impolite.

"Now what a thing to say." She shook her finger at him as if he were a naughty child. "Pennington, I'd like you to meet Jonathan, the love of my life."

Jonathan moved closer to shake his hand, noticed that the skin on his face and neck was loose, hanging in tiny drapes. His hand was enveloped by Jonathan's. *He is old and slow and tiny. No way he can stop me.* "Glad to meet you, Sir." Jonathan pulled out his charm card and played it, "This is a nice place you've got here. A little far from town, though." He forced a laugh.

"Yeah, town is not a good place for me to try to get around. I drive in and do my bank work and pick up prescriptions at the pharmacy, both at drive-through windows, then I get a burger at another drive-through and I come on home. My truck has all hand controls, makes it real nice."

Jonathan tried not to look at Penny's shrunken legs, and just nodded his head.

"Come on in, Helen's fixed us a bite for supper. Let's eat and then we'll get y'all settled in." Penny led the way through the house, swinging one leg and steadying himself with the other bent leg, crutches scraping and squealing as he moved. Most of the house was darkened with drapes pulled, but in the dining room the curtains were tied back and they caught the soft evening light.

"Thank you, Helen. Come and meet Naomi's latest, Jonny, I believe she said was his name." A young woman came from the next room drying her hands and tucking a stray strand of hair behind an ear.

"Pleased to meet you, Sir."

"She helps out here in the afternoons," Penny explained. "Cooks and cleans and takes good care of the house."

She could take good care of me, too, Jonathan thought as he imagined her young form through the loose t-shirt and jeans she was wearing. "The pleasure is all mine, Young Lady."

Naomi scowled, "We can take it from here. Helen, you can go on home. Thank you." Helen looked at Penny who nodded and she disappeared quietly.

A hearty meal of hot bread, roast beef, mashed potatoes, green beans, and creamed corn was steaming on the table, and the three ate well.

When Penny finished he leaned back and laughed, "I guess you are clearing the table, Naomi, and washing the dishes."

"What on earth, Penny? I have no intention of cleaning up."

"Well, you sent the cook home early, so I figured you were wanting to wash dishes tonight." He chuckled. "Jonny Boy, no one can accuse my sister of spending too much time in the kitchen."

"Oh, Penny, really." She threw her napkin on the table, rose slowly and flounced out of the room.

"She can be a pain, my sister." His eyes followed her path out of the room until he heard the front door slam. "But I expect you know that already."

Jonathan was unsure how to reply, so he just nodded and helped himself to more mashed potatoes.

Penny chuckled dryly. "I expect you are smarter than the last man she brought here. Must be to leave that line untouched. Ahh, my little sister. What did she tell you, that she was ignored as a child? That I got all the attention? I believe she told that last fellow something about, let me think, that her first husband abused her. Did you get that version?"

Jonathan was listening, fork loaded with potatoes poised in the air. *What the hell? Am I being conned? Nah. I must just be tired from the drive and paranoid about this creepy old house and this strange little man.* He cleared his throat and set his fork back on the plate. "Naomi has never been anything but honest with me, I am sure." He shoveled in the bite of food.

Penny threw his head back and whooped. "Well, you are loyal, I give you that." He pushed back from the table and struggled to his feet. "If you want to check out the farm in the morning, I've got a sweet tractor, hydrostatic transmission, you know, so everything works with hand controls. Just holler at me in the morning if you want to take a spin." He winked as he shuffled through the room.

Jonathan sat alone in the big dining room, thinking about all he'd seen and heard today.

While Jonathan sat pondering his next move, Penny joined his sister on the front porch. "Why do you have to get rid of this one? I kinda like him. Citified, but with possibilities. He's smart."

"Hush," Naomi spoke with clenched teeth, "look what he did to me." She pulled her knit top down at the neck with two pincher-like fingers." He whistled.

"Owie, why did you sit still for that?"

"He said that he was going to have one, too, with my initials in it," she whispered watching the door.

"Well, didn't he?"

"No, he tried to fool me with a fake one, but he forgot to draw it on the night we spent together. I was sick, but I am sure about that. He has no brand. Nothing. And he might have tried to poison me that night. I was completely out of it." She crossed her arms and rocked in the chair beside her brother. "I am completely done with him."

Chapter 42

"Okay, then, he's got to go. All the papers in order?"

"Yes."

"What does he have?"

"Nothing. This isn't business, it's personal." Naomi rocked more forcefully.

"Okay, whatever you say. Thank you again for bringing a little excitement into my life. Afterwards, we must actually deal with the pipeline lawyers. Good thing we did a yield assessment on the well before the pipeline came through. The case will be cut and dried."

The door squeaked open and Jonathan peeked out. "I'll go get the luggage, Dear, where must I put it?"

"Straight through, first door on the right," Penny looked from side to side and found their serious faces quite humorous. "Cheer up, kids, and get some rest. Tomorrow is another day."

Chapter 43

Fishing

That same evening, Stella got a phone call from Jonas. "Hey Babe, we are back early. Stormy weather. Wait 'til you hear what I got. Since we bailed early, Captain Bob is giving each of us a free ticket for a half-day fishing trip anytime this summer. Isn't that great?"

"That is real nice, great." She could not even muster up fake enthusiasm. "I'm on my way."

Might as well give him a few more minutes of peace and quiet. He's not going to believe this. Timmy Lee has not gotten in this much trouble before, except maybe for when he killed that man.

She replayed the scene with Margaret earlier in the day. The shock of what Margaret told her was still with her. She said she was an undercover private investigator for the family of Naomi's last husband. It seems that Naomi had had five previous husbands and one boyfriend dead or missing. Margaret was worried about Jonathan, who was really Timmy Lee. Stella hadn't known what to do or what to hope for, but Margaret took over and got it started. She had gotten the Pence Springs address earlier from Naomi, and contacted the Pence Springs city cop who brushed her concerns aside. He actually told her that he wasn't going out to the farm because it was not in town so not his jurisdiction, but she could call the state police.

"Let me call Elmer. I should have done that first, since I promised I would." He'd answered quickly.

"Elmer, that car is owned by Timmy Lee's girlfriend, and they are heading your way."

"Where exactly, Stella, your place?"

Chapter 43

"No, to the family farm, uh, Rutherford's in Pence Springs." She gave him the address. "They should be arriving early this evening. Oh, and Timmy Lee is going by another name, Jonathan Wesley."

"Stella, what crimes have actually been committed?"

"Murder, Elmer, suspected murder, remember? And the woman is under investigation for multiple murders. She may be gonna kill Timmy Lee."

He thought about that for a few seconds. "Looks like this could all work out for the good of humanity, Stella. Let's give it a day."

She wanted to hang up but she didn't. "Are you joking, Elmer?"

"Yeah, about halfway. As soon as I have a spare deputy, I'll send them over there to do a safety check on the both of these characters. Might as well pick them both up and get to the bottom of this. Is Jonas back yet?"

"No, Elmer, you have to deal with me. I'll have him call and confirm what I've told you as soon as he gets here." She was angry that her information was not good enough, and this time she hung up on him.

Margaret asked her to keep her identity secret. She had a contact in the South Carolina state police to call next, but Stella needed to get outside, she needed air. They agreed to stay in touch during the next few hours.

After Stella's call, Elmer doodled on his desktop calendar where he had written Jonathan Wesley and Rutherford. He made a note to send Deputy Long over when he got back from his current call.

* * * * *

Stella swung the truck into the parking lot of the marina and picked up her exhausted husband. He stashed his fishing gear in the truck bed. "Do you mind driving, Hon?"

"Glad to."

"Did I miss anything today?"

Stella laughed off her nervousness. "It can wait until after you eat, Jonas. Pick any fast food to-go window." She waited until they were at home at the condo, the last burger wrapper was crumpled into a ball and the last French fry was eaten, and then she told him about the day's events, nervously, with big pauses to let it sink in.

"So, do we need to leave tonight?" Jonas did not look ready to go anywhere, reclining on the couch, sunburn starting to shine on his face and arms.

"I don't think so, Jonas. In fact, why do we need to go at all? If somebody needs us, won't they call?" Stella was sitting perfectly erect, hands folded primly in her lap.

"And you think that he's going to be picked up tonight?"

"Yes, according to Elmer. I forgot, Jonas, the sheriff wanted to talk to you. You know how he is sometimes. He needs to hear things from a male voice to take them seriously."

Jonas grinned, "Stella, you have driven him fairly crazy in the last few years, he and I have known each other for three decades, we are pals. I'll call him right now."

"Humph." She wandered away to straighten up the kitchen, even though there was little to do since it was unused today. She wanted to call Tisha and Eliza and Jonas's mother in Alaska, but was just too tired to go through it all again. She'd call when Timmy Lee was safely behind bars.

Jonas wasted no time. "Hey Elmer, Stella said to give you a call."

"Thanks Jonas, did she brief you on Timmy Lee's possible location?"

"Yes, sir. Have your men picked him up?"

"Well, about that. Deputy Long is still out on a domestic disturbance, so looks like it will be first thing in the morning. We don't have any idea that he is leaving soon, do we?"

"No Sir, but I sure will feel better when he is in custody."

"We'll get him in the morning, Jonas. Get some rest. I'll call you as soon as we have him."

"Thanks, man. Good night, Elmer."

Jonas and Stella didn't sleep well. Stella opened the sliding doors so they could hear the waves, but even the lullaby of the waves didn't lure them to sleep. The real reason was that for the first time in a long time, they knew for sure that Timmy Lee was on the prowl.

Chapter 44

Tractor Lesson

Naomi was dressed for sleep and in bed by the time Jonathan came out of the bathroom. Variations of hope in the form of getting rid of the other person danced in both heads. *This is the last night I have to pretend to care for you, old woman,* repeated in Jonathan's head whenever he had to summon up something nice to say. Every time he spoke, Naomi thought, *you despicable phony.*

Jonathan slept on the edge of the old bed, and Naomi curled into a ball as far from him as she could. Neither slept well and the bed creaked each time they moved. Early the next morning, Jonathan gave up trying to sleep and tiptoed out of the room and down the hallway to grab some coffee and something to eat. Penny was already up, sitting at the kitchen table. "Hey there, Jonny. How'd you sleep last night?"

Chapter 44

The sound of the old man's voice startled Jonathan. *I have to get a grip*, he thought.

"Make yourself at home, Boy. Coffee's on the counter, just pick a little cup there and pop it in the machine. There's donuts in the cupboard over there and eggs and bacon in the fridge if you want to cook."

Jonathan stuck a coffee packet in the automatic brewer and found a donut and wrapped it in a paper towel. He leaned against the counter waiting for the coffee to finish.

"You look like you been rode hard and put away wet. Didn't you sleep well?"

Jonathan shook his head, wary about even speaking.

"Cat got your tongue?"

"No." Jonathan ventured a word and grinned, then took a bite of his donut.

"Never saw a preacher that ate without giving thanks to the Lord. You must be one of them progressive church men." Penny's eyes twinkled. "But let's talk about today. Are you interested in riding around the place? I can't take you, the tractor only holds one, but I can give you directions. You ever handled a tractor before?"

"No, Sir." Jonathan was not very interested in riding a tractor around, but a plan was starting to take shape. "Can it dig?"

"Boys always want to dig with their toys, don't they?" Penny grinned and clapped his hands together. "Yes, it will. I'll show you where the controls for the backhoe are. There's a picture right there on the tractor, nothing to it."

Jonathan, mouth full of donut, nodded.

"There's a place on the other end of the farm, about a mile away with all the twists and turns, where there is loose dirt that would be easy to practice digging." He took a drink from his coffee cup and seemed to be amused. "There's an old logging road that you can drive on, I'll sketch out a map. On second thought, just follow the logging road. I'll show you. That would be a great way to see the farm, goes right past the livestock pens and the big barn then up a ways where the view is real pretty."

"About that loose dirt, are there houses nearby? I mean, I wouldn't want to disturb anyone with the noise. Tractors are fairly noisy, aren't they?"

Penny leaned back in the kitchen chair, "Not a soul for miles, you can dig to your heart's content."

"I think I'd like that." Jonathan chugged his coffee. "Do you have time to show me this morning?"

"Nothing I'd like better." He grabbed his crutches and pushed himself upright. "I'll go check the gas, I think it was topped off last week." He looked out the window. "It'll lighten up quickly – you can hear the early morning birds at this time of day. Beautiful outing. Wish I could go with you." Jonathan heard him chuckling all the way to the back porch.

Jonathan snuck back in the bedroom and grabbed a pair of khaki pants and a long-sleeved shirt. He put them on and carried a pair of socks and deck shoes with him as he left. Naomi did not move.

He sat in the kitchen and finished dressing. He was excited. He could avoid Naomi and solve the problem of her disposal all in one morning. *Should probably dig a hole big enough for them both,* he figured. He bounced up and joined Penny just beyond the backyard where he'd pulled the tractor around. Penny gave him the operating instructions and Jonathan practiced going forward and backward and lifting and lowering and tipping the bucket.

Penny pointed out the entrance to the logging road, yelled, "You have fun, Boy, life is short," and shooed him away, waving and laughing.

Penny stood at the back door and watched the man and tractor grow smaller then disappear into the woods. He lurched back to the kitchen and thoughtfully resumed his coffee sipping as he looked through a file titled "Water Testing." The only sounds in the room were the regular ticks of the clock on the wall and the random slurps of coffee from his cup.

It was daylight when Naomi finally joined him, dressed in a pink plush robe. She sat down slowly. "I just don't know how I'm going to do it, Penny. In fact, it's giving me a headache."

"The problem may be solved any minute, Girl." Penny cupped a hand around his ear as if he were listening.

"How?" She looked around. "Where is Jonathan? I heard y'all out back earlier with the tractor." At that moment, the house shook with a mighty boom.

Pictures fell off the wall and dirty dishes left on last night's dining room table came crashing off. The old man was thrown against the table and Naomi's chair flew backward into the wall. They both ended up on the floor. Sounds of breaking glass continued after the motion stopped, and dust and dirt rained through the air.

Chapter 44

"Good Lord, Penny. What was that?" Naomi crawled over to him. He was face down on the linoleum, his body shaking. His silver crutches glistened in the heavy dust, scattered across the kitchen away from his body. "Penny, Penny, are you all right?" She crawled to him and reached gently to turn his face in her direction. His eyes were closed tightly and he continued to shake.

He tried to speak, "Jonny." He coughed and tried again. "That man, Jonny." He rolled over on his back and held his stomach.

"Are you hurt, Penny. Is it your stomach? Let me look." She peeled his hands from his midsection and felt for injury.

"Not hurt." He stopped shaking, opened his eyes and took a deep breath. He smiled at her. "I expect it was the love of your life that caused that explosion."

"You are laughing? You old fool." She pushed his side and crawled away, throwing anything in her path at him as he lay there laughing again. "What explosion? Where is Jonathan?"

"Help me up and I'll tell you all about it."

Chapter 45

After the Boom

Calls reporting the explosion poured into the Pence Springs Police Station, the Summers County Sheriff's Department and the West Virginia State Police Headquarters. Even the Monroe County Sheriff's office had gotten a few calls, and Elmer took a deputy and drove over to investigate himself.

There was a blue State Police helicopter hovering over the site by the time Elmer got there. Firefighters had been on the scene and white Mountain Top Pipeline trucks were arriving. Several outbuildings including the big barn had been flattened and some had burned. The nearest neighbor, nearly a mile away, was in bed, hung over, and would've missed it if an overhead shelf hadn't fallen on him. The next nearest neighbor was Penny Rutherford. He was missing and feared dead.

Elmer took it all in, then quizzed a state trooper standing by with a clipboard. "Do we know what caused it?"

"Pipeline exploded, best we can tell. Don't know why, maybe those guys can explain it." He raised his chin at the pipeline men.

Elmer wanted to see the site for himself, so he sought out the Summers County Sheriff, Bob Fleeman, and volunteered himself and his deputies to go with Fleeman to help out at the accident's location.

"Sure, Elmer, glad to have a couple of extra pairs of eyes. Firemen have finished and cleared the way for EMTs. Don't know about survivors that close to the explosion. May not be much to see – hey, you have a camera with you?"

Elmer did and sent for it from the car.

Chapter 45

Fleeman stopped the group of law enforcement officers and spoke, "Listen up, if you see anything out of the ordinary, let's get a picture and a location. Carl here will take notes and one of the Monroe guys will take the photos. Jim, do you have the evidence number tags?"

"Affirmative, Sheriff."

They trudged up the access road, seeing nothing of interest until black burned streaks appeared, getting more widespread until the ground, still smoking, opened up into a wide, shallow crater. Firefighters in full gear were finished and taking off helmets and getting bottles of water.

The brush was scorched several hundred feet from the pipeline, and Elmer went to do his own exploring. He carefully parted the smoldering branches and followed the burn path. He found a skeleton of a burned machine lying on its side and called, "Bob, c'mere and take a look at this."

"I believe that was a tractor," Bob speculated. "Looks like it got blown over here and then burned. It's still warm. Reckon anybody was on it?" They looked it over carefully. Fleeman was thoughtful, "I reckon we'll need to scrape it and let the lab boys work on it. If somebody was on it, they never saw it coming. There are worse ways to die, huh, Elmer?"

Elmer had wandered off again looking through the charred ground. His voice was gentle, "Bob, I got something over here." He pointed to an oddly shaped mass, burned black. "Might be a pelvis, Bob. We are going to need to hand search this area an inch at a time. Hard to tell how far things have been blown."

Bob nodded and called the uniformed men and women together. "This here is now a fatality investigation. We need to organize and send for more equipment and some four wheelers to get evidence out of here." He continued to bark orders while Elmer walked away. He had a phone call to make.

Chapter 46

Identification

"We could do a DNA swab and see if the remains are Timmy Lee," Elmer gently explained to Stella. "You don't have to look at this mess."

Stella had thought of nothing else since the phone call two mornings ago. She and Jonas had packed up the truck, sloppily, but fast. She blew a kiss to the ocean and turned the keys in to the realty office in hopes the salespeople could re-rent it the rest of the week and refund their money.

She'd called Margaret when she got home and told her that Naomi had arrived back in West Virginia. Margaret then reported her news, "Obviously, Naomi is not here. Penny's housekeeper has reported to the West Virginia State Police that he was missing, but not a word about Naomi. I am afraid that Naomi has gotten by with murder again. I am so sorry, Mrs. Akpik."

"We are not for sure yet that it was my brother," Stella was firm. "Shoot, it could even be an ole cow, it was burned so badly. But, thank you. Anyway, I expect he meant to do harm to that old woman sooner or later." She couldn't bear to say or even think "Good riddance" if it was him. *People probably wouldn't understand.*

* * * * *

She waited on a wooden bench with Elmer and Jonas at Charleston's Forensic Lab where the remains had been sent. They were waiting to be called in.

Jonas was flustered. He twisted around to look at her, "Stella, you don't have to do this. Elmer is right. Timmy Lee has put you through enough pain. Get the swab done, over in 10 seconds, and let science decide."

"No can do, Jonas." She shook her head, jaw locked and teeth gritted. She had other plans.

Just then the inner door opened and a man in a white lab coat came out. "Mrs. Akpik?" She nodded. "I am Dr. Tariq Rana. We are ready, but I need to let you know that this experience may be intense. If you'd like to leave at any time, you may. There is a bathroom just outside this area, beyond the door to your left. If you have questions, please feel free to ask. Is there anything you need to ask now?"

"Do I look through that window?" She pointed.

"Yes," he nodded. "I'll raise the shade and you can take as much or as little time as needed. This is a particularly difficult identification. The body, or actually the body parts, have been badly burned." He looked at the three of them and then back at Stella. "Okay?"

"It's show time." Stella walked to the window to wait for the shade to rise. Jonas stood behind her, but he looked away after the shade rose and the sheet covering the body parts was pulled back. Elmer remained on the bench, looking at the floor.

"Well, that could be just about anybody." She studied every bit and part of the body, her eyes staring at the head and shoulders the longest, but she couldn't see hair or features, just a flat-faced black head, mouth open. The feet were in pretty good shape in comparison, but the legs and arms were mostly charcoal. Then, she saw the hands, burnt claws from where she stood.

She rapped on the window and the doctor returned. He asked kindly, "Have you seen enough?"

"No, I need to come in there and look."

Elmer moaned, "Oh, God, no, Stella."

Jonas held her upper arm. "Honey, are you sure?"

"Well, I'm not doing this for fun. I want to be sure, Jonas." He was pale. She softened her tone. "You don't have to come in with me. This doesn't bother me a bit."

She entered the room, smelled the strange chemicals, noticed how clean the corners were. That's where she always looked first in a new place. She was so in tune with her surroundings and herself that she tasted the waxy surface of her lipstick and smelled its fragrance. The cooling unit in the room kicked on and startled her. Then her movements seemed to her to be in slow motion.

She moved around to the back of the table to see his right hand. The fingers were attached and seemed to be relatively intact. She let her eyes trace the middle finger's length. *The middle finger was shorter. It was him.* She gasped and recovered. *Now, what do I do?* She answered silently. *If I tell the truth, then we have a funeral or a memorial service. Sure won't be a celebration of his sorry life. Then we have to bury him or have him cremated. Should get a discount on the cremation,* she snorted and then coughed to cover it. *He will be a victim of an explosion and the pipeline has probably budgeted for loss of life, so we'd get a settlement or maybe his son would. That would give him the last laugh, for sure. On the other hand, with my luck, they'd prove the explosion was his fault and we'd have to pay them for damages. His name would be in the paper and the news people would dig up ... "* She laughed silently at her own pun, mouth covered with a tissue, *" ... his past, probably interview Jonas's mom and aunt and video us in our grief. But, if I say it is not him, I am done with him forever. No funeral, no bills to pay, no respect for the dead, no marked grave. Just done.*

Dr. Rana cleared his throat.

Oh, Lord, he wants me to decide. "Just a few more moments, please." She tried to look sad, to squeeze out a tear. She could mimic the fast triple sigh that happens after crying a lot and she summoned one of those up. After another minute or two, she nodded and the doctor took her elbow and led her out.

"You can come into the office to complete the paperwork." He guided her through another door, Jonas and Elmer following behind in single file. They found seats while Dr. Rana seated himself at the desk and opened a folder.

"Can you identify the deceased, Mrs. Akpik?"

Stella looked at Jonas when she answered, "No, I cannot."

He looked up with wide eyes. "Are you quite sure? You did spend a good bit of time studying the remains."

"Yes, Sir, quite sure." She said with a nod. Dr. Rana seemed surprised.

"We are done here, then?" Stella looked around at the men and stood up to leave.

"Just a minute, I want to thank you very much for coming in." Dr. Rana stared at her as if he could read her mind. "Could you share with me your thinking?" He wanted to talk more but Stella was done.

Chapter 46

"I'm sure. It wasn't him. I would know my own brother."

"Can you use dental records?" Jonas had been prepped by Elmer, who knew about such things.

"No." Dr. Rana shook his head. "We don't have enough left."

"DNA?" Jonas asked.

"Not likely. The remains are badly burned and DNA may have been contaminated externally."

Jonas had no more ideas. He shrugged and thanked the doctor. Stella was out the door before he rose to shake hands with Dr. Rana. She seemed too overcome with emotion to say goodbye. Jonas gently took Stella's elbow and walked beside her to the parking lot, Elmer following.

Once inside the truck, Jonas muttered, "Then who could it be?"

The sheriff spoke up from the back seat. "All I understand right now is that I need a drink. I know a place. Y'all want to come?" Elmer looked weary.

Jonas looked at Stella who nodded. "We're in."

Two hours later, after five beers apiece for the men, Stella announced that she was driving. They didn't argue. "Stella, are you pos-i-tive-ly sure it wasn't Timmy Lee?" Jonas was loosening up.

"Skootch in here so I don't have to talk so loud. Elmer, you, too." She looked around outside their booth and lowered her head. "I'm only going to say this once and I will forever after deny saying it now."

She made them look at her before she spoke. "That charred pile of parts was my brother, Timmy Lee Davis, as sure as I'm sitting here."

"You lied?" The beer had made the sheriff bold.

"Off the record, Elmer?"

"Of course," Elmer slurred.

"Yes, sir. Cause I didn't like him enough to even respect him dead. And I got to decide whether he had a marked grave or a funeral or a death certificate or his name in the paper. It would've been awful and this isn't real kind, but I picked my poison, Jonas, and I will live with it."

Dead silence descended on their booth for a full sixty seconds. Then Jonas whooped, "Ain't she something?" He looked at Elmer and threw his arm clumsily around Stella.

The sheriff leaned back and closed his eyes wearily. "Remind me not to look too hard for the poor fellow who was killed."

The sheriff laughed so hard, he doubled over and put his head down on the table.

"Or for Timmy Lee," Jonas added and they both burst into gales of laughter again.

Stella rolled her eyes, but neither of them noticed. She prayed silently, *Go rest high on that mountain or wherever you ended up, Timmy Lee. And God, I'll see you in church tomorrow. We have some catching up to do.*

Epilogue

Margaret (not her real name) left the nursing home and went back to her work as a private investigator. She visited nearly every weekend and dealt a few games of Rummy for her friends each week. Nurse Danvers shook a finger at her and laughed whenever she saw her.

The suspicions of the family of Naomi's last husband were confirmed when his remains were found under the flattened barn on the Rutherford place.

Penny Rutherford's and Naomi Waterman's bank accounts were emptied the day of the explosion. Naomi was the subject of a search that rattled Pence Springs and the residents of the Sea View Nursing Home in Myrtle Beach, South Carolina, but she was never found. The girl that helped Penny left the area a few weeks later and the rumor was that she joined them out west.

Mountain Top Pipeline never made any money. The Pence Springs explosion and others during their first months effectively bankrupted the company. Judges ordered the monster pipes removed from the land, but by then, MTP did not have the funds to comply and the pipes rusted where they were. A three-hundred-mile-long depression in the ground and the missing trees were the only damages left behind. Stella and Jonas planted an orchard on their easement and replaced the oak trees that were cut down.

Elmer and Jonas and Stella kept Timmy Lee's death a secret as long as they lived. It bound the three of them together even stronger than their friendship had been before, but none of them ever spoke of it again. They all thought about him from time to time, though, especially Stella.

She and Jonas lived together in the farmhouse until they were well into their nineties, traveling far and wide, taking in stray dogs and relatives, and loving each other. Tisha and Eliza and their children helped them move into a nearby assisted living facility when they were both in their mid-nineties, and visited often. Jonas fought cancer long and hard before his death at age 98. Stella was able to go to the Bradley Cemetery for his services.

She shooed her friends away and stayed afterwards, balanced on a walker, to talk to Jonas and her friend, Anna. She whispered to them both, "Save me a seat. I'll be along soon," and blew them kisses before she summoned help to get her to the car. She ordered the driver to return her to her farmhouse after the funeral, and she lay down in the big cannonball bed. She murmured that she would die there, and she did, within a few days.

At her funeral, there was a large framed picture of her in the tree so many years before and a favorite quote by Laurance Rockefeller, "How we treat our land, how we build upon it, how we act toward our air and water, will in the long run tell what kind of people we really are."

The farm and small estate were willed to one of Anna's great-granddaughters, a social worker, to provide foster care for animals and runaway girls.

The local newspaper headline read,"Retired Monroe County Writer Obstructs Pipeline Route with Car."

Story by reporter Charles Boothe, The Bluefield Daily Telegraph.
Photo courtesy of Appalachians Against Pipelines.

About the Author

West Virginia educator and author Becky Hatcher Crabtree enjoys rural life on her beloved Peters Mountain in Monroe County, West Virginia. Her life experiences influence her writing, especially this year as eminent domain was used to take part of her farm for a gas pipeline. In this story, her main character, Stella, faced some of those same issues. In actuality, Becky sat chained to a 1971 Pinto, her first car, across the pipeline path in a short-lived attempt to slow construction. She notes that Stella may have handled the problem with more sense.

Becky and her husband, Roger, tend to a menagerie: a small herd of sheep, two dogs, chickens, a cat, and one fainting goat. They have three daughters: Papi Jeanne, Katherine (Katie) Rebecca, and Dinah Dale. They also have five grandchildren: Isabel, Elizabeth, Clark, Gabriel, and Rachel.

www.ingramcontent.com/pod-product-compliance
Lightning Source LLC
Chambersburg PA
CBHW051132020726
47501CB00005B/1472